BE EVER
HOPEFUL,
HANNALEE

Behave Yourself, Bethany Brant
Charley Skedaddle
The Coach That Never Came
Eben Tyne, Powdermonkey
(coauthored with Phillip Robbins)
Eight Mules from Monterey
Jayhawker
Lupita Mañana
Sarah and Me and the Lady from the Sea
Turn Homeward, Hannalee
Who Comes with Cannons?

BE EVER HOPEFUL, HANNALEE

PATRICIA BEATTY

MORROW JUNIOR BOOKS
NEW YORK

Printed in the United States of America.

3 4 5 6 7 8 9 10

Library of Congress Cataloging-in-Publication Data
Beatty, Patricia. Be ever hopeful, Hannalee.
Summary: In 1865 with the war recently over, fourteen-year-old Hannalee and her
recently reunited family decide to start a new life in Atlanta where, because of the
need to rebuild the devastated city, jobs are plentiful. Sequel to "Turn Homeward,
Hannalee."
[1. Reconstruction—Georgia—Fiction. 2. Atlanta (Ga.)—History—Fiction.
3. Family life—Fiction] I. Title.
PZ7.B380544Bd 1988 [Fic] 88-21581
ISBN 0-688-07502-9

To
Faye Evans Dunkle
—— *and* ——
Maxine Tate,
book lovers both

Contents

	Preface	1
Chapter One	Davey's Decision	5
Chapter Two	On Our Way	18
Chapter Three	The New City	30
Chapter Four	A Real Bad Place	47
Chapter Five	"Not Fast Enough by a Long Shot!"	62
Chapter Six	"Hannibal Sanders"?	75
Chapter Seven	Some Salvations, I Reckon	87
Chapter Eight	Atlanta Living	100
Chapter Nine	Delie	115
Chapter Ten	Caught!	128
Chapter Eleven	Worse Than War	142
Chapter Twelve	Help?	156
Chapter Thirteen	Decatur Road and Beyond	168
Chapter Fourteen	The Scuppernong Cave	180
Chapter Fifteen	We Do Things!	193
	Author's Note	208

Preface

THE NOVEL PRECEDING THIS IS *Turn Homeward, Hannalee*. Although the characters in it are fictional, much of it is based on Civil War facts.

Turn Homeward, Hannalee begins in July 1864, with the cavalry troops of the Union Army attacking northern Georgia. The Reeds were a family of mill workers in the town of Roswell. By the summer of 1864, the father, a Confederate soldier, has recently died of illness in an army camp. The mother is pregnant so can no longer work, but Hannalee, who is twelve, and her brother Jem, nine, can. Hannalee is a bobbin girl who carries yarn and thread on bobbins to the weavers, and Jem is a lap boy who feeds the raw cotton into a special machine. The oldest son, Davey, in his twenties, is a Confederate soldier in the Roswell Guards.

Just before the Yankee soldiers descend on Roswell, Davey, who is home briefly on leave, quarrels with his sweetheart, Rosellen Sanders. He refuses to marry her then because he doesn't want to leave her a widow if he dies in battle. After the quarrel he goes off to war again.

I

When the Yankees come, Hannalee, Jem, Rosellen, and hundreds of women and children are gathered up by the soldiers, held in the town square, then sent north by train to the Ohio River as "traitors" to the Union because they made tent cloth and rope for the Confederate Army.

On the train journey Hannalee attempts to disguise Jem as a girl by cutting off her long hair and having him wear her braids stitched to a sunbonnet so they can stay together. But Jem later refuses to be disguised.

In Louisville, Kentucky, Hannalee, Jem, and Rosellen are split up when Northern people hire them as workers. Beautiful Rosellen is a very skilled mill hand and goes to a mill in Cannelton, Indiana; Jem goes to a Kentucky farm; and Hannalee becomes a maid-of-all-work in a Yankee household in Louisville.

Hating her work and her Confederate-despising employer, Hannalee runs away. Able to disguise herself as a boy because of her now short hair, Hannalee makes her way to Indiana to find Rosellen. Rosellen gets Hannalee work in her mill under the name of Hannibal Sanders, and a good home with a pleasant Yankee lady who teaches Hannalee that all Northerners are not evil.

Hannalee longs for home. She tries to get Rosellen to head back to Georgia with her, but, still angry at Davey, Rosellen refuses to leave her work. Besides, she is friendly with the Yankee mill owner's son—too friendly to please Hannalee.

Alone, Hannalee leaves Indiana for Kentucky. On her way to find Jem she runs into the Confederate bushwhacker Quantrill. Seeing his cruelty firsthand, she learns Confederates can be evil, too. She finds Jem, and he is as eager as she to run off home.

Though frightened at their boldness, they start out through Kentucky and Tennessee. In Tennessee they are witnesses to the terrible Battle of Franklin, a Confederate defeat. Passing through the lines after the battle, they are told by a soldier that their brother Davey's regiment was badly mauled in Virginia and that he must have been killed. A grieving Hannalee uses her elementary knowledge of the alphabet to write Rosellen that Davey is dead. That way, she reasons, Rosellen can truly begin a new life. She does not know if the letter will ever reach Rosellen, though.

Hannalee and Jem make their way to Georgia any way they can travel—on horseback and by riding with a sympathetic peddler.

They arrive the day after Christmas to find their house was burned by Yankees and their mother is now living with Rosellen's old aunt, Marilla. Mrs. Reed has had her baby, a girl named Paulina. Hannalee and Jem do not immediately tell their mother that Davey has been killed. The words stick in their throats. Though Roswell has Yankee soldiers garrisoning it, Hannalee and Jem are not arrested. Because the mill has been destroyed, there is no traitorous work for any mill hands.

The winter of 1864–65 is a cold and hungry time for the Reed family.

The war ends with Atlanta burned and much of Georgia ravaged by the Yankee Army under the leadership of General Sherman.

June 1865 comes, and with it a knock on their door. Davey enters. He was not killed in Virginia. He was wounded, captured, and had to have part of his left arm amputated in a Union Army hospital. Discharged after the war, he has come home. He was a mill carpenter and plans to go to the nearby city of Atlanta to help rebuild it and make himself and his family a new life.

Hannalee has the sad duty of telling him that his true love, Rosellen, is lost to him. He seems to accept this loss calmly, but Hannalee knows it has wounded him deeply. Yet two things can be said: The war is over, and they are all together again.

The second book about Hannalee Reed and her family begins the same month that Davey came home—June 1865.

CHAPTER ONE

Davey's Decision

JUST AS I STARTED LOOKING OUT THE WINDOW of the room I shared with Aunt Marilla on that hot June night in 1865, the fireflies came. They came suddenly—the way they always do. First there was a black sky, then there were hundreds of gold and yellow lights sparking up the darkness. I took to fireflies, liking to watch them flick on, then off. For the longest time I just wouldn't believe there wasn't anything to them but little flying bugs. When I was real small, I had liked to think they were fairies with wings dancing in the air. Now that I was almost fourteen, of course, I'd had to put that notion behind me. It was as if the fireflies had showed up on purpose this very night, our last night in Roswell. The little lightning bugs had come to say farewell to us Reeds, who'd lived here ever since I'd been born.

I wasn't feeling exactly fine and dandy right now. That was for two reasons. First was because we were leaving Roswell to satisfy my big brother Davey's hankering to move us all to Atlanta.

Second was because I'd met up again this very morning

5

with Sulene McPhee, an older mill girl whom I'd never liked. She'd run smack dab into my little brother, Jem, and me on the street. Having been dragged away north last July by the Yankee soldiers, same as Jem and me, hadn't sweetened her nature much.

Sulene came sashaying up to us Reeds, her long, brown, red-ribboned pigtails swaying. As soon as she spied us, she'd stopped in her tracks, clapped her hands over her mouth, and gawked at my short hair. I'd cut it off to try to disguise Jem as a girl to keep us together up north. It had grown out some but wasn't quite to my shoulders yet. I was always wishing it'd get a move on and grow faster.

When she took her hands down, she'd cried out, "Hannalee Reed, don't you look a fright, though. You look like a boy, not no girl I ever seen."

Although my cheeks were burning, I pretended not to hear her. I eyed her up and down, thinking that she looked pretty good. Sulene had some meat on her bones, which was more than we did, and she had a new yellow calico dress. Her eyes weren't so big in her face as mine and Jem's. That meant she'd been eating proper.

I asked her, "Did you just get home from the North? I ain't seen you in almost a year. Where'd you get took?"

She'd frowned at my question and said, "I got put to work as a spinner up in Kentucky, workin' to make Yankee-blue cloth. They fed me real good where I lived. My mill was a old wooden one that could take fire real easy, so I was glad when the war was over and I could leave it and come home."

Jem told her, "You could have run off from the Yankees, like we did! How'd you get here? Did you walk, too?"

"No, I had me some money I earned, so I come on the railroad far as the line went, then I walked here. Wasn't far. I only got here yesterday. Ma and Pa were sure glad to see me finally. I had a Yankee lady write 'em I was comin'." Sulene's face had changed then. "I see our old mill ain't started up yet."

I'd said, "No, it ain't. Mebbe it never will, since the Yankees busted it up."

Jem burst in with, "Our old mill don't matter to us Reeds no more. We won't ever work in it again. Our brother Davey's takin' us all to Atlanta tomorrow."

"*All* of you?" She'd started to grin, a twisted, wicked smile. "Your ma and the two of you and Davey? How 'bout Rosellen Sanders, Davey's sweet, true love?"

Oh, I knew what devilment she was up to. Sulene had always been jealous of Rosellen's beauty and fancy ways. And, of course, she'd have asked her folks about Rosellen right off.

I picked my words with care. "Rosellen didn't come back with Jem and me. She's fixin' to come back here later on." This was a lie because I knew in my heart Rosellen wouldn't come home. This mill girl wasn't going to hear that from me, though.

Sulene went on grinning. "That ain't what I heard. I heard she ain't never comin' home, 'cause she's got a Yankee lover by now. Davey'll have to find hisself a new sweetheart."

That was all I could stand to hear from her. I knew she sort of fancied my big brother herself, so I'd said, "Davey Reed can have any pretty girl he wants—he's that handsome in his face and ways. Come on, Jemmie. We got errands to run for Mama and Aunt Marilly."

I'd walked so fast getting away from that sassy mill girl that shorter-legged Jem had to trot to keep up with me. He'd told me, "I bet that old Sulene's jealous we're goin' to Atlanta—Davey and me and the baby and Rosellen's Aunt Marilly."

I'd said, "Mebbe so, Jem. Don't you mind about her. Sulene McPhee allus had it in for us Reeds, 'cause Davey favored Rosellen over her."

We quit talking about Sulene after that, and walked in silence for a few minutes. Suddenly Jem said, "Hannalee, won't it be fine for us in Atlanta, though?"

"I surely hope so, Jem," I'd told him.

I'd taken a look at his face and noticed how his eyes were shining. He looked at moving to Atlanta as a great big adventure, but then he was always ready for an adventure. I'd had my fill of adventures last year!

And now it was nighttime, our last night in Roswell. I was remembering Davey's coming home just five days ago. As I watched the fireflies popping in and out of sight in front of me, I thought hard on him. Mama hadn't heard from him once since he'd left for the war last summer— not one word.

And then, without any warning, he'd come to the door of old Marilly Sanders's house where we'd lived since the bluebelly soldiers had burned our house last July. Davey had knocked and there he was—but he wasn't the Davey Reed we used to know. This one was thin and ragged and hungry and—worst of all—one-armed. He'd been wounded and was put in a Yankee Army hospital where half of his left arm had been cut off to save his life. It wasn't until he was strong enough to walk all the way from Virginia that the Yankee doctors had let him go.

After we'd laughed and cried over our surprise at seeing him alive, it had been my painful duty to tell him Rosellen had decided to stay on as a well-paid drawing girl who set the patterns in the cloth at the mill.

As a firefly came close enough so I could reach out and touch it if I had wanted to, I told myself I thought I knew what it was that drove him to want to leave Roswell. It wasn't only that Atlanta had jobs for one-armed carpenters like him but also because it didn't have any hurting memories of Rosellen.

But Roswell had memories for me—good ones of the

days before the Civil War! I remembered Pap here, before
he'd died of camp fever in the army, and I could remember, too, seeing Davey working in the mill repairing
looms—working with two good, strong arms.

All at once I heard somebody laugh under my window.
Not Davey. It was a man's laugh, though, probably one
of the Yankee soldiers still stationed here in Georgia to
keep an eye on us Southerners. Georgia men didn't laugh
much these days after being whipped in the war after four
long, dreadful years.

I heard Marilly walking slowly up the steps to come to
bed. Mama and Paulina, my new baby sister, who was
born last year after Pap had died, were already in bed in the
other little room across the hall. Davey and Jem had gone
out to say farewell to some menfolk we knew.

Marilly, the white-haired lady us Reeds loved, had lit
her way up to bed with a candle. Because I'd turned the
kerosene lamp way low to admire the lightning bugs, she
didn't blow the candle out once she'd opened the door and
come inside. She set it, still burning, on the top of her
chest of drawers.

I said to her, "Mebbe I ought to write Rosellen one
more letter and tell her Davey ain't dead, after all, that he's
come home to us. I could ask her to come home, too. The
preacher's wife'll help me with the letter, 'cause I don't
write so good yet."

The old lady sat down on her bed and began to unbutton her shoes. With her head down she said, "If my niece came back and then married up with Davey on account of your letter, he would allus think she done it out of pity 'cause he's only got one arm now. Let her think on him as dead. It's better for both of 'em that way, Hannalee."

Because it was hard for her to get her shoes off, I took the buttonhook and knelt beside her. Her wrinkled hand came down to stroke my hair. It was pitch-black, like my eyes, and came from Mama's Cherokee blood.

"Your hair's growin' out, and you're shootin' up to be tall like your pa."

I nodded. As I hauled off one of her high-buttoned shoes, I asked, though I knew beforehand what she would say, "Mebbe Davey could stay here in Roswell to help build up what the Yankees burned down?"

"No, Hannalee. He needs to go to Atlanta and take us with him. He takes bein' the head of the family mighty serious. He claims they're jest cryin' for carpenters in Atlanta. He's dead set on goin' there."

I sighed and told her, "I'm glad you changed your mind and will be comin' with us, Aunt Marilly. Nobody I know your age is half so spry as you be. Us Reeds will be honored to have you live with us in Atlanta when we been livin' with you for near a year now."

"It's been a joy to have your comp'ny here." Marilla's voice broke a little. I looked up at her as I tugged on the other shoe and saw by the lamp's yellow glow that tears glittered on the white, stumpy lashes of her closed eyes. She mumbled, "I'm ready to go. It ain't as if I got anybody anymore to wait around for here, and at least I still got Sanders kinfolk there, last time I heard."

"Aunt Marilla, we're your fam'ly now, long as you can put up with our ways."

"I can do that. Now help me braid my hair for bed, and then help get me undressed. I see you've got on your nightgown already. What were you up to on your knees at the window? Prayin'?"

"No, I already done that. I was watchin' the lightnin' bugs."

"Were you now? I used to like 'em, too—such a surprise they are when they come blazin' out of nowhere. I heard tell there ain't no fireflies way out in the West. Go back and look at the bugs. It's cooler at the window. I can undress myself and braid my hair."

I went back to the window and kneeled down again, thinking about Atlanta. It wasn't too far from Roswell, after all. I'd gone there once with Pap before he went into the army. What a big city it had been—lots bigger than our little town. What would it be like now after the Yankees had captured it, too, the way they had Roswell?

I blew out Marilly's candle and turned off the flame of my lamp. In the darkness I looked once more for the fireflies, but they were gone. The night was black. They'd said their good-byes to me, just as Davey and Jem were doing in Roswell right now. I should have gone with them, but I didn't have the heart to pretend I was glad to leave.

I wondered what Mama was thinking about our leaving here, where she'd married Pap and the four of us kids had been born. She was part Cherokee, and sometimes her Indian blood told her things about the future. Would it have anything to say about our going to Atlanta?

Before breakfast the next morning I went in to see her while she nursed Paulina. Mama's window was open, and I could hear Davey's and Jem's voices from where they were sitting on the front porch. They must have got up at day-peep, or never went to bed at all.

Mama said, "Don't they sound fine, though? Jest like they used to sound. Now, if you only had your long, pretty hair, Hannalee." She bit her lip, thinking, and added softly, "And Davey his other arm."

I nodded. "Mama, what does the Cherokee in you have to say about goin' to Atlanta?"

She looked sharply at me. "Davey wants to go, Hannalee. He *needs* to go."

"I know. He's rarin' for it, and so's Jem. What about you, Mama?"

She shifted Paulina to her shoulder to pat her back. "Is somethin' botherin' you about Atlanta, Hannalee?"

"Yes, Mama. Us Reeds have old-time friends here in Roswell. It's Davey's idea to go. It ain't yours or mine."

"Child, there's money to be made in Atlanta now—

good money." Mama handed the baby to me and swung about, putting her feet on the floor. "Davey needs to think he's head of our fam'ly now. I don't want to take the heart out of him by disputin' him over this. I want better for us than we can get here. You stand a better chance of goin' to a real school in Atlanta. I want a house of our own; I don't like bein' a burden on Marilly. Davey aims to get rich fast. I dunno that he will, but we got to be ever hopeful that good will come out of this—no matter what does come. I know you came a far ways to get home here to Roswell, and you think kindly on it 'cause of Pap. Think on Atlanta this way: Us Reeds'll be together there. Wherever we'll be, that'll be home to us, won't it?"

"I reckon so. Are there mills there?"

"I don't know. I don't want any of us workin' in any more mills, though, not tendin' to looms or fetchin' bobbins. There ain't no way to get ahead in that work, and it's bad for folks' lungs. Lint gets into 'em the way it did to your pap. It weakened him and helped to kill him of sickness. Goin' to Atlanta will mean gettin' out of the mills, and that's what I aim for. Your pap's life and mine—for years it was only the mill here. Gettin' into mill work is easy. Gettin' out can be danged hard. Davey and Pap would still be there if the war hadn't taken 'em as soldiers. Mebbe it done some good, after all."

Knowing her feelings, I didn't have the heart to tell her

that I was wary of going to another strange place that would be raw and new to me.

While I sprinkled cornmeal into boiling water for our breakfast mush, I talked with Davey and Jem. I could tell from the way my big brother held his head and said that he wasn't hungry that he'd been drinking corn whiskey the night before. I took it as strange that Roswell folks who were living on cornmeal, greens, and hominy now—because the bluebelly Yankees had stripped Georgia clean of pigs and sheep and cows—would have whiskey in their houses. Aunt Marilly said it was because the whiskey gave poor Georgia people the courage to go on. It seemed to me they'd given plenty to Davey.

As I stirred the thickening mush I asked, "When'll the wagon be comin' to take us to Atlanta?"

Mama and Marilly and I had already packed up the things we'd be taking. It wasn't much, because the Yankees had burned just about everything we owned. Aunt Marilly was taking some pots and pans and furniture, but that was all. Plenty of folks would want to move into this house she'd paid rent on for years.

Davey muttered, "My head feels big as a punkin. I surely sampled a number of jugs last night. Will Tucker's wagon'll be here around nine. It's a big one."

I told him, "I can see you got an offer of a jug or two, Davey. And I bet you never once said no to one."

"I didn't, Hannalee. One hand can hold a jug jest fine while a man drinks from it."

"Did any of the Yankees here in Roswell stop you because you got drunk?"

"Nary a bluebelly pestered me. It ain't as if I was with a group of our Confederate cavalry. All it was, was me."

Mama came down now with Paulina, and Aunt Marilly followed after her to set the table for our mush. All at once I was ashamed of my sharpness to Davey about the whiskey.

I looked at him, seeing how his hair gleamed black in the rays of sunshine from the open kitchen door. My heart hurt for him, making me forgive him for his farewell drinking. Thin as a slat, he still wore his gray and butternut-brown uniform. He would have to wear it till he got some new duds somewhere. His old civilian clothes had been burned up with our house.

It would gladden me to see him out of uniform. I was dead weary of Yankee blue, but weary, too, of Confederate gray. The war was over, and though like every other Georgian I grieved at our losing it, I still rejoiced at its being ended.

When Davey filled out more, he'd surely catch the eyes of some Atlanta girl who'd put Rosellen out of his mind for good. That would be the tonic for him: another love. He had a way with the ladies. They came on to my brother like honeybees to blossoms in the summertime. I just hoped he wouldn't be unlucky in love again. For sure that might take the heart right out of his breast. Whatever I could do to keep him free of more pain, I surely would do.

It wouldn't do me any good to talk with him, telling him how I had worries about our going to Atlanta. He wouldn't want to hear me. He needed to get away to a new life.

Well, I knew lots more about making my way in the world than I had last year. I'd stood up to lonesomeness and homesickness, and here at home to being hungry and cold and suffering heartaches over him and Pap. I reckoned I'd be all right in Atlanta, and, like Mama had said, I'd try to be hopeful.

As I spooned the yellow, gritty mush into bowls, Mama poured cups of what we called coffee from the big pot. It was mostly chicory, and as bitter as could be.

Though he wouldn't eat, Davey did take a cup of that. He swallowed deep and shivered at the taste. Then he cried out as he lifted the cup again. "Here's to Atlanta! By the start of 1866, us Reeds will have hung the moon way up high in the Atlanta sky, and I'll be on my way to bein' a rich man."

I caught the strange look that suddenly crossed Mama's face, and I knew from it that her Cherokee blood had just told her something that didn't comfort her. The look on her face hadn't comforted me!

CHAPTER TWO

On Our Way

THOUGH WILL TUCKER'S WAGON WAS BIG, IT WASN'T BIG enough for Marilla's belongings, her, and all us Reeds, too. So most of the time on that hot June day, Jem, Davey, and I walked beside the noisy wheels in the dust of the road. To save our shoes—the only ones we had—Jem and I walked barefoot. After all, it wasn't as if we weren't used to using our feet. All three of us had walked hundreds of miles in the last year. Besides, Atlanta wasn't far—only twenty or so miles south of Roswell, a good day's traveling.

I couldn't say I enjoyed what there was to see along the way. There were mostly bluebelly Yankees on the road with us, and every one of them seemed to want to see the passes Mama, Marilly, Davey, and Mr. Tucker had had to get in Roswell for us to travel at all. When the bluecoat soldiers came toward us, either marching or riding horseback, Will had to take the wagon to the edge of the road, then wait to show our passes and let the Yankees pass by first, before we could move along. That was what Yankee soldiers expected. Though the war had been over two months, Georgia was still swarming with bluecoats.

Although I looked as hard as I could, I didn't see any of the bluebellies robbing farms and houses along the road. I said to Davey, "They don't seem to turn off the road to get what they can from the houses and farms no more."

"No," he agreed. "They already been there. They already got what they could get out of these parts. Ain't you seen the burned-out houses and torn-down fences and fields gone to weeds and brambles we been passin' by?"

I nodded. I'd noticed them. Before the war came to Georgia, this had been a pretty part of our state. I remembered it from the time Pap and I went to Atlanta so he could see a doctor about his lungs. We'd gone there by train, but there wasn't any railroad anymore. The Yankees had taken up the rails all over the state, so our army couldn't move quickly from place to place or get the things they needed to help them fight—cannons and cartridges, food and clothes. The bluebellies, cuss them, had sure been hard on our railroads. They had pulled up the iron rails and heated some of them till they were red-hot, then twisted the metal around trees. Some wooden ties still lay on the side of the road.

Sometimes we sang as we walked along. Davey or Mama would start up "Lorena" or "Lily of the Valley" or some other song we all knew the words to, and we'd sing along. Jem and I weren't blessed with good voices, but Mama had a sweet, low one, and Davey a true one for the high sounds. I took note, though, that nobody ever started up "Aura Lee," the song that had been Davey and Rosellen's special one. It's strange how some songs with memories tied to them went to a person's heart and stayed there. I'd never hear that one without remembering yellow-headed Rosellen Sanders and wondering how she was faring way up yonder in Indiana. Had she married up with some Yankee there? Mama had heard that some Roswell mill girls had.

As we passed the breast-high, red-dirt ramparts that our Confederates had built in a ring around Atlanta, dust rose up all around us. It'd been a mighty dry spring and summer so far. The dust came from the other wagons we had started seeing. They came out from little side roads to join us. A number of wagons had sacks of greens in back. Many were stacked high with fresh-sawed lumber. Others carried firewood.

Being a carpenter, Davey took note of all the wood we were seeing. He told me, "There won't be many trees left standin' around Atlanta by the time it gits built back to what it was. With so many folks comin' in to the town, they'll be needin' firewood, too."

I nodded. I'd seen more and more tree stumps as we neared the town. I hated seeing the stumps. I liked trees. "What'll it be like in Atlanta?" I asked him.

"It'll be busy, Hannalee. Atlanta allus was a busy place. It's fast time there, faster'n ever now. Take Richmond in Virginia. Atlanta ain't one bit like Virginia

towns I saw. Those are real old places. Atlanta ain't half
so old as old Marilly."

That took me by surprise. Marilly claimed she was past
seventy but wouldn't tell anybody how far past.

"Do tell!" was all I could say, thinking of how big
Atlanta had seemed to me when I'd gone there with Pap
before the war. Five Points, the middle of town, was the
busiest place I'd ever set eyes on, and how tall the brick
buildings were—some of them three stories. I couldn't
believe then that there could be so many horses and carriages and wagons in all of Georgia.

Davey took off his gray soldier's cap to cool his head.
"Atlanta started up about forty years back as a place to
trade with Indians, and it growed from that to be the spot
where four important railroad lines come together. Think
how busy one line can make a place when a train comes in.
You traveled north by train, so you know somethin' about
'em."

"You bet, Davey." I'd never forget the Yankee trains
Jem and Rosellen and I had traveled on for hundreds and
hundreds of miles. Sitting on those wood benches had
made for mighty sore hindquarters.

As he swatted dust from his butternut shirt, Davey
went on. "Atlanta was all-fired important in the war."

Jem came trotting back to us from where he'd been
walking alongside Will Tucker and caught the last of what
Davey had been saying. "Why was it so danged important,
Davey? Was it more important than Roswell and our mill?"

"It sure was." With his one hand Davey roughed up Jem's hair, black as his own and mine and Mama's. Our little sister, Paulina, was the only one of us Reeds who had Pap's red hair. "Our Roswell mill made tent cloth and uniform cloth and rope. Atlanta had foundries to cast cannons and rolling mills and factories that turned out pistols and iron plates to put over the hulls of Confederate navy ships to keep off Yankee ships' cannon shots. Atlanta made a heap of things that kept the Confederacy and the war going."

I asked, "Was that why that old Yankee devil Gen'ral Sherman did such wicked things to it?"

"You bet, Hannalee. That's why he busted it up and burned some of it down—so the Confederacy couldn't get supplies from it anymore."

"Davey, if it hadn't made guns, would he have destroyed it?"

"Probably not. He might have took food stores and whatever else he had a need for, and then moved on to some new town. He kept movin' through Georgia to the ocean after he burned down Atlanta."

I shivered in the hot weather, thinking of the news that had drifted back to Roswell of Sherman's march through our state to Savannah. Folks claimed he left a fifty-mile-wide swath through Georgia as bare as an apple tree after a November windstorm.

"Don't look so down in the mouth, Hannalee," Davey

said. "It ain't as if Atlanta's goin' to look all busted up the way it was when Sherman left. It's risin' truly fast to be a city agin. It ain't a town that can be kept down long—not Atlanta."

I looked at him and saw him grinning at me. He was happy. Mama had saved our carpenter's tools whcn our house was burned. They were in a box in the wagon not twenty feet from us right this minute. Last time I'd got up into the wagon to rest, I'd sat on the box. Not wanting to be a "croaker," a whiner, I grinned back even though I just couldn't get the strange look I'd seen on Mama's face this morning out of my mind. Her Cherokee blood had for sure told her something!

After a few more minutes of walking, I ran ahead a little to Mama and Aunt Marilly, who were sitting on the wagon box next to Mr. Tucker.

I asked Marilly, "Where did you say them kinfolk of yours live in Atlanta?"

She was fanning herself with an old kerchief because of the heat and dust. "I don't recall exactly, honey. They ain't my kin, but my poor dead husband's. It wasn't on Peach-tree Street or Washington Street, where the real rich folks live. It was on the south side of town." She nodded. "I'll know the house when I set eyes on it, though. Zilphey lives there with her husband, Jace, my husband's brother, and their boy, whose name I plumb forget. I'll know where to turn off to it when we come to Peachtree Street."

I didn't ask her more about the Atlanta Sanderses because she'd said she hadn't seen or heard from
them since her husband died over fifteen years ago. He'd
had a spat with his brother. According to Marilly, Jace
Sanders had become a clerk in a bank, so he thought he
was better than a Roswell mill hand, which was what her
husband used to be. I couldn't help but wonder if the Jace
Sanderses would be glad to see Marilly after so long a
time. They hadn't written one word to her in all these
years. It appeared to me Marilly might not be too welcome.

No matter if she wasn't. She'd be with us. Us Reeds
didn't ask favors of anybody. We shouldered our own
way through the world. As Pap used to say, "The heavier
the load, the brighter the crown." Look what we'd come
through in the war—us losing Pap and Davey losing his
arm; Jem and me on the road to home for so very long;
and Mama birthing Paulina alone with no loving Reed kin
nearby. The night Davey came home, Mama had said that
she thought he and Jem and I had hung the moon in the
sky. That was high praise, and hearing it had pleasured me
no end. Now, I sure hoped and prayed her three offspring
would do so fine in this new town that she'd say those
same words again before the year was out. No matter
what I'd be called on to do, I'd do my share.

Whatever it was that had gotten Mama's Cherokee
blood a-going, she must have felt down inside her that

we'd do all right in Atlanta, or she would have given Davey an argument about going. She would have won out over him, too. Nobody could stand up to her when she wanted her way. I was glad she didn't want it often. Right now she knew Davey needed Atlanta to heal his mind and get back his pride. That was something menfolk had a great deal of. Our Confederate men had sure been hit hard in theirs. I could see it in the way most of them in Roswell sat and slumped and walked weary-like. I could see it in their faces that didn't smile and their eyes that looked past me like they were staring at something far-off. There was a stillness to them—less talking, too. It appeared to me they'd gone as gray as their uniforms—like they had ashes in them. Underneath there could be red coals still afire, but I hadn't seen that. Yes, Davey was acting more full of life now than other Georgia men, but I'd sneaked looks at him in Roswell, and I'd seen that he acted like all the others.

Not the Yankees, though. Although the soldiers stationed in Roswell generally didn't strut around like barnyard roosters, a few did. They didn't lord it over us, and we Reeds weren't bedeviled, but I could read the look on Yankee faces that said, "We won the war, so don't you Rebs give us any trouble." Because they ate well, they filled out their blue uniforms. Their brass buttons were shiny, and so were their boots and horses. I tried not to hate them because it wasn't the proper thing to do, but I did dislike the bluebellies a lot all the same! The Yankee lady I'd lived with up in Indiana had turned out to be nice, but Yankee soldiers? Nosiree! The faster they took themselves out of Georgia, the better!

Davey had told us they were hanging around because the Yankees were afraid us Confederates would start fighting them again, and they wanted their army to be on the spot to stop us. Georgia was under what they called "martial law," which meant the Yankee Army was the law in the state and had the power of life and death over us.

As I was walking and pondering bluecoats, a bunch of them came up behind us, riding fast. There were two wagons abreast on the road and no place for the cavalry to get through, so their officer hollered out, "You people, get those wagons out of our way right now!"

Will Tucker got his scared mules over to the side onto some grass, but the other wagon, which was pulled by one skinny horse, had to take to the roadside ditch where it almost turned over. After the Yankees galloped past down the empty road toward Atlanta, Davey, Jem, and I ran over to the wagon in the ditch. Will Tucker gave Mama the reins of his mules and got down to join us. He jerked on the horse's bridle to get it up, and the three men pulled and pushed to get the wagon free.

And then we started on our way again. We were almost to Atlanta by now. I could see the spire of a church in the distance, and knew this was the city. It was good to see a church spire. Aunt Marilly and Mama set great store on churchgoing, so they'd expect us all to go to one once we got settled in.

I was hoping to hear church bells soon, so I asked Davey, "Did you hear any church bells when you came through Atlanta on the way home? Our minister's wife in Roswell grew up in Charleston. She said there was nothin' prettier than a whole lot of church bells ringin' out on a Sunday mornin'. Our mill bell in Roswell wasn't nice-soundin' at all."

Davey gave me a sharp look, then a laugh. "Hannalee, I doubt if there's a church bell in any steeple anywheres in the South right now. They all got melted down to make cannons during the war." At my unhappy look he added, "Don't fret. Once Atlanta gets goin' good agin, there'll be church bells for you to listen to." Now he frowned. "I dunno, though, about how the churches done durin' the time Atlanta got shelled by Yankee big guns. I didn't take note of 'em 'cause I was so set on gettin' home fast as I could. I didn't mosey much around the town—only enough to see it was buildin' up agin. I know for a fact that the artillery used church steeples and other high things as shootin' targets. Mebbe churches got hit, too."

I sighed. That was just like Yankees to shoot at churches! I said, "Our Confederate gunners wouldn't ever do that to a Yankee church."

Again Davey laughed. "Don't you be so sure they never did. Our men wasn't so finicky on their way north to

Gettysburg, Pennsylvania, back in '63. Now don't look like you don't believe me! What I tell you is true. There ain't no cause for you to be a fire-eater now, honey. The Yankees is here. Atlanta'll be full of 'em. They'll be thick as fleas on a bluetick hound's rump. The best thing to do is act so they don't take no notice of you. Don't give 'em any sass."

"I didn't give 'em any in Roswell."

Jem, who was listening in, added, "I didn't neither, Davey. Mebbe they knew we was mill hands escaped from Yankeeland, but mebbe not. Everybody who knew about us kept real quiet. Anyhow, they never came to grab Hannalee and me and ship us back north. They could have done that."

Our big brother nodded. "They could have if they had a mind to. I got to admit the bluebelly doctors and nurses who looked after me in that hospital in Virginia done good by me—as good as they would have done to any soldier from their own army. They couldn't save my arm, but they surely did try."

I bit back tears, looking at Davey's sleeve, pinned up to cover the stump of his left arm. I cried whenever he talked about it, and it pained me when I could see by his tightened lips that it was paining him. That stump was something he'd never let me or anybody else see, and I didn't want to, neither.

Now he said, "I didn't do so bad with one arm

haulin' that wagon out of the ditch, did I, little sister?"

"You did jest fine, Davey."

He didn't say anything else for a few minutes. Then he went on with something I'd been waiting to hear. "Hannalee and Jem, you done right not tellin' Mama you figured I was dead 'cause of what that soldier up in Tennessee told you. There wasn't any cause to make her grieve. I'm glad you waited."

I told him now, "I wish I hadn't wrote to Rosellen that you got killed. I was too hasty. I could have waited. Mebbe she never got my letter. The war was still goin' on then."

"No matter. That's all behind us now. Rosellen, too. We'll be takin' on a new life as city folk."

"You bet!" shouted Jem, who danced a little jig, raising up even more dust.

CHAPTER THREE

The New City

O H, WHAT A CHANGED PLACE ATLANTA WAS FROM THE town I'd visited with Pap!

You could hear the city before you really got inside it. It wasn't so much the noise of wagon wheels and horses' hoofbeats and people calling out to each other as the sounds of hammers nailing boards together and saws rasping away. All those hammers going at once made my ears ring, so that I wanted to put my hands over them.

Davey yelled into my left ear, "See what I told you! Ain't it fine the way Atlanta's buildin' up so soon agin?"

Just before we headed downhill into town, past burned-down houses that were mostly only a wall and a chimney, Mama motioned for us to come over to the wagon. She pointed to our shoes, hanging around our necks. She wanted Jem and me to put them on before we entered the city. Decent folks wore shoes in town. Mama had her pride.

And then we went along with lots and lots of other folk into what Pap had told me was called "The Gate City." Never in my life, not even when I was in Louisville and

Nashville last year, had I seen so much commotion and moving about. Folks were walking, riding horseback, or riding in carriages and wagons. Everybody seemed to be in a hurry, too—not smiling or laughing or gawking or waving at each other.

Looking about, I could see Yankee soldiers in blue; ladies in fancy, bright-colored, hoop-skirted dresses; whiskery men in frock coats and high silk hats; and lots of freed black people walking about. The black people were dressed about the same way us Reeds were—in calico and homespun. So were quite a few white folks—people who weren't rich, either. I couldn't help but note that the look on Southern folks' faces here was livelier than in Roswell. Though they didn't smile, their eyes were sort of lit up like they were thinking bright thoughts.

Sweating men, some in butternut-brown shirts, were at work everywhere I turned my eyes. They were carpentering and sawing, pushing wheelbarrows, carrying bricks in a wooden contraption on their shoulders, and mixing pasty gray mortar in wooden troughs. Buildings were going up as fast as they could be built. I saw wooden ones that were just finished. Others appeared half done, and a lot were only wood frames.

A hive of bees! That was what Atlanta reminded me of, but instead of buzzing, there was hammering and pounding and yelling. As we passed by a building that was only a frame so far, I looked through its timbers to what was behind it. There was only a weed-filled lot with two brick walls standing in it. I could see black marks on the walls, which meant there'd been a fire. Beyond the lot, a distance away, there were other plots of ground that either had rubble on them of what had been buildings or just plain dust and emptiness. One place I saw wasn't anything more than a flight of five stone steps going up to nothing at all. It looked strange. What had been here before the Yankees came? Somebody's store, I reckoned, because this was the commercial part of Atlanta.

Nosiree, this town didn't look much like the fancy Atlanta I'd seen with Pap. It was all tore up for sure. From where we were walking, there were hardly any three-story buildings to be seen at all. I remembered how the blue-bellies had blown up our mill in Roswell last summer. They were good at destroying property that didn't belong to them, and it appeared to me that they'd been hard at it in Atlanta, too.

I glanced at Davey. His eyes were sort of sparkly as he looked around. He liked the noise. Jem seemed to like it, too. He had his head up high, like he sniffed something good to eat on the dusty breezes. Not me, though! I don't cotton to messes, and that's what Atlanta looked like. I don't like things that are being built or made half so much as I like them finished and done with. I'd taken note that men were different from women that way. They liked the fuss and noise and busyness, and once they were done with something, they looked around for the next thing to do. That's how it had been in our mill. As soon as one new kind of cloth pattern was finished, the menfolk started right in on the next one. Mama sometimes said that no man who was ever born knew how to let well enough alone. He'd always be fixing or changing. Pap had been like that. So was Davey. It was in his nature.

There were so many wagons and carriages around us now that I had to stand on tiptoe to spy out Will Tucker's. Whatever happened, we mustn't lose sight of it. I got Jem by the hand and hauled him through the carriages, dodging horses and wheels over to where Mama sat. A glance over my shoulder showed me Davey was pushing his way through, too. I figured it wouldn't be so easy to do with only one hand and half of one arm, but he was doing fine. I'd taken note in Roswell, though, that he didn't seem to balance himself so easily as he used to. Once he'd been the best dancer in town, and I wondered if he still would be, but there hadn't been any more dances in Roswell after the war.

Mama had to shout down to us. "Marilly's remembered where her husband's Atlanta kinfolk live. It's called Edgewood Avenue. Will Tucker says we got to turn around and head north, then go east. You keep close behind the wagon so you don't get lost, you hear? I never saw so many folks or heard so much ruckus in all my days."

Paulina started to wail, and Mama tried to comfort her by rocking her in her arms. As for Aunt Marilly, she had her ears covered with her hands so she wouldn't have to listen to old Mr. Tucker's cussing about how he'd have to turn around.

He couldn't do that right off. He had to turn off into a street of ruined houses before he could find a clear place to swing the wagon out of the way of other wagons. Then we were back on Peachtree Street again, with me looking for peach trees but finding none. I figured either the Yankees or the Atlanta folk had hacked them down for lumber and firewood.

After a while Will Tucker turned right onto the street I reckoned to be Edgewood. As we went down it, the street appeared to me to be in almost as bad a shape as Peachtree Street. There wasn't so much building going on here, and more houses were standing, but a lot of them looked mighty poor. Some had no roofs. Others had great big holes in their walls so you could see right through them.

It was quieter here, too, so we could make ourselves heard without hollering.

Davey caught my arm and pointed to a house that was nothing more than walls with big holes in them and a tall redbrick chimney. He said, "That's what cannon fire does. A cannonball or two went right through this house."

I gasped. "With folks livin' inside?" These buildings weren't stores but places to live in.

His not answering told me what I already reckoned to be the evil truth. It wasn't just soldiers that got shot at.

He said instead, "I heard tell the bluebellies shelled Atlanta for forty-six days with cannonballs and with shells that set fires. They're called incendiaries."

I trembled. I was sure glad Roswell wasn't shelled like that. What had happened when the Yankee cavalry had come in had happened fast—in a couple of days, not forty-six of them. Living in Atlanta then must have been sort of like living in Bible times with the forty days of God's raining. It'd been bad enough for all of us in Roswell, of course, but nobody had shot cannonballs at us. Different towns got different treatment from the Yankees. Some caught it worse than others. Atlanta had given the bluebellies trouble in holding out, and it'd gotten paid back for it.

"Davey, Hannalee, Jem!" came Mama's cry as the wagon stopped in front of a white house surrounded by a picket fence that was missing most of its pickets. Something else was odd. There was a vegetable garden in front where flower gardens generally were.

I heard old Marilly say, "Yes, this'd be Jace's house. I recall the yellow jasmine on the front porch. I wonder if Zilphey's at home."

Davey told her, "There's only one way to find out. I'll go and have myself a look."

Without being asked, I went along with him. We would

have gone up to knock on the front door, but when we stepped onto the veranda, we saw that the door was nailed shut, with nails pounded into the frame. Davey left the veranda and went along the right side of the house past the rows of cabbages and carrots.

What a big surprise we got when we went out of the yard. There was hardly any house at all behind the front! There was some roof left at the rear over what appeared to be a patched-together room, but the middle of the house behind the front had fallen into a big heap of boards and bricks.

"Oh, Davey!" was all I could say.

He wasn't paying me any heed, though. He stepped over the boards and called out, "Jace Sanders? Miz Zilphey Sanders? Is there anybody here?"

Though it didn't appear so at first, we finally saw somebody. A tiny, gray-haired lady in a faded, rose-colored calico dress came out from somewhere in the rear part of the house. She asked sharply, "Who'd you be? I haven't got nothin' to give you or to get stolen. What do you want?"

Davey took off his gray army cap to be polite. "David Reed from Roswell at your service, ma'am. I fetched your kin, Marilly Sanders, here to you."

"Marilly?" The woman sounded surprised.

I asked, "Are you Miz Zilphey who's wedded to Marilly's husband's brother?"

"*Was* wedded. Jace got hisself killed in the bombardment one night," she said, pointing to the busted-up part of her house. "He wouldn't go inside the pit when I asked him to go. He said, 'The devil with the Yankees,' and jest sat there by the window. The shell didn't kill him the way it did Dr. Byer on this street. Flyin' glass from the window done that, so Jace bled out his life when it didn't have to happen."

I told my brother, "Let's get Aunt Marilly back here."

Zilphey asked, "What brings her here to Atlanta?"

I explained, "She came with us. My brother here's a carpenter by trade. There ain't no mill work in Roswell for us, so he's come here to work, and he fetched us and Marilly along with him."

Now Miz Sanders wanted to know, "How come she's here with you? Is she kin to you folk?"

Davey said, "No, ma'am, but she's kin to Rosellen Sanders, the girl I came mighty near marryin' before she got sent up north."

For a moment the woman was silent, then she said, "That's right. Jace had another mill hand brother, and he had a girl child. Don't fetch Marilly here. I'll go around to the front to speak with her. I hope she don't have it in mind to move in on me. There ain't room, and there ain't food enough. I may be goin' to the Freedman's Bureau the Yankees run here and ask them to feed me the way they feed the blacks. I may not have a house no more, but I don't aim to starve."

I asked, "Are the bluebellies handin' out food to anybody that needs it in Atlanta?"

"They are. It'll gall me to go to 'em, but I will."

Davey spoke as cold as ice. "We never will! I been hungry. All my kin have been, but we didn't beg food from bluebellies."

I almost told him how last winter Jem and I had gleaned corn that had fallen from the mouths of Yankee horses in Roswell. The bluecoats had let us, and that dropped corn had made us cornmeal good as any gotten from a store or a field. It'd galled me to glean from a horse, and to ask to do it, but I had.

Zilphey Sanders went inside the room that was still standing and came out with a straw bonnet on her head. She led the way out over her busted-up boards but walked to the left, not around to the right. She pointed to a hole in the bare dirt. The opening went down, and on top it was partly covered up with sawed boards.

"That's where I holed up when the Yankees shelled us. Jace dug it, and I fixed us up a bed and kept candles and water down there. When they fired their big siege guns at us durin' the day, we went about our business. I cooked and cleaned, and Jace went to the bank. But when the Home Guards wouldn't take him to go fight the Yankees because of his bad back, he got so ornery, he quit joinin' me in the hole."

She gave one of the top boards a little kick with her foot, turned to us, and said, "You, David Reed, it's plain to see you were in our army and got wounded.

How about the rest of you mill folk? I heard tell the bluebellies came to little Roswell before they came to Atlanta."

From her voice I could tell Aunt Marilla had been right about the Atlanta Sanderses. They did look down on mill hands. I said, "They did come there first. We had a hard time, too—real hard."

"Did the Yankees cut off your hair, girl?"

I'd forgotten I'd pushed back my sunbonnet a while ago to enjoy the breeze and cool off some. "No, they didn't. I did it for a reason. Miz Sanders, it's hot here. Marilly's waitin' in the wagon." I'd spotted a well and dipper and asked, "Could we all have some water?"

"Why not?" She had a rough laugh. "It doesn't cost anythin'."

And off she went with Davey while I walked to her well to haul up the bucket and fill the large dipper. First, though, I drank, enjoying the cool water as I felt it go down my dry throat. Our trip had been a long and dusty one. My arms were sunburned where my sleeves didn't cover them.

With the dipper brimming in my hand, I picked my way around the far side of the old mules to where Marilly and Zilphey were talking together. Jem and Davey leaned on the wagon's side.

Because she was the oldest one, I gave the dipper to Marilly first. She drank deep, then passed it on to

Mama, who passed it to Mr. Tucker, who gave it to Davey and Jem.

While we all drank, I listened to Zilphey Sanders say, "You say you got a gold piece, Marilly? Well, that's good. The only money that can pass around here these days is Yankee greenback paper money, gold, and silver. Confederate money ain't no good at all anymore. I warn you, though. One gold piece won't go very far at all. You'll be needin' a place to live. Rents are high as a cat's back. They say that out of the four thousand some buildings that were here in Atlanta a year ago, that cussed Yankee devil Sherman left only about four hundred standin' when he marched out of here last November. Fires he had set did that mostly."

Marilly said, "We're sure sorry to hear about Jace, Zilphey. I understand why you can't take me in, but I never planned on that. I'm stayin' with the Reeds. Where can we go to find a place to live?"

Zilphey let out a little sigh. "North of town, Marilly. There's a camp there for folks who've been burned out or have just come to town. Lots have come here from the country—white and black folk. The camp for the blacks is at the south end of the city on Decatur Road. The one for white ones is to the north. It'd be smart to keep away from Decatur Road and the camp there. They say there's smallpox there among the black people. It's real bad. Even the Yankee doctors don't mess much with smallpox, though I hear they try to keep it from spreadin'."

I could tell that the talk between the two old ladies was almost over. Aunt Marilly had said there wasn't much love lost between the two of them. The dipper was empty, and Jem handed it back to me. Because I'd fetched it from the well, I figured I should be polite and take it back, say "Thank you" to Miz Zilphey, and wish her well. It didn't appear to me that she wished us well, but she'd had a lot of pain in the war, too, and she hadn't had so much family as us Reeds had.

I remembered about her son and asked her, "Didn't you have a boy, ma'am? Aunt Marilly said she recalled you did."

Mama said, "Oh, Hannalee!" Not knowing it, I'd done something bad.

Miz Zilphey's face crumpled. Then she said, "Our dear boy Tom was with Gen'ral Cobb's troops and got killed at Fredericksburg two years ago."

I'd heard of that battle. General Cobb had got killed in it, too. I said, "Oh, ma'am, I'm sorry to hear that."

Mama said, "Hannalee, Miz Sanders told us that jest before you got here with the dipper. Now take it back and we'll be on our way."

I started for the well, but as I did, I felt Zilphey's hand on my arm. "It wasn't your fault, child. You didn't know."

All I could say was, "Our pap died in the war of sickness—camp fever, it was."

She nodded. Then all at once she shaded her eyes with

her hands to look east down the street. She cried out to us just as Will Tucker finished hoisting Marilly back up onto the wagon seat. "I see Amalie's wagon. She'll be stoppin' here. She always does."

"Who's she?" asked Marilly. "Kin of yours?"

"Yes, she's a Redmond. Maybe her brother Gar's drivin' today. No, it's only Amalie. There's durn little Amalie can't do."

We waited till the dark green wagon with gold pictures on its side neared us. Over its top I read the gold letters: CONFECTIONERS. I had trouble with that word because I'd never seen it before. What was a confectioner, anyhow? Before I could ask Zilphey, the wagon, pulled by a gray horse, was beside Will Tucker's.

I nearly popped my eyes like a frog staring at the driver. "Amalie," Miz Zilphey had said. Amalie Redmond was so pretty, she took my breath away—maybe even prettier than Rosellen. I'd never cottoned to red hair, but Amalie's wasn't carroty or strawberry blond. It was a deep red, like the color of cedar wood, and it shined and curled around her face. Her skin wasn't the freckly sort that generally went along with red hair, but pale and soft like white rose petals. Her big round eyes were such a bright hazel-gold that they bore into you. She wore a checkered yellow-and-white gingham gown and a white straw bonnet with yellow ribbons. The hands that held the reins wore yellow gloves. How elegant she was! She made Mama and me look dirt poor in our dull calico dresses made out of the bolt of unbecoming dark blue cloth Marilly had saved at the start of the war.

This lady pulled in her horse next to the rickety old wagon and said in a low, soft voice, "Aunt Zilphey, I fetched you a basket of food." She looked curiously at white-bearded Will Tucker and us Reeds. Then her glance fell on Davey, who'd come away from the wagon wheel to stand in the middle of the road and look up at her with his hat off. When she saw him, she smiled. Her smile was like the sunrise in summertime. She'd sure taken note of him—and he of her. What man wouldn't?

He said, "I'd be Davey Reed from Roswell. We jest came here for a minute so Miz Marilla Sanders could visit with Miz Zilphey, and now we'll be on our way."

The lady nodded. "I'm Amalie Redmond. My brother, Gar, and I are in business here in Atlanta. Sometimes I come out here to see my aunt. Corporal Reed, would you give her this basket, please?" She reached down to her feet and hauled up a woven basket with a white cloth over its top.

Davey came forward to take it, then brought it over to Zilphey and set it at her feet.

Miz Zilphey didn't ask her kin to get down and visit, and I wondered at that. She said, stiff as a ramrod, "Thank you, Amalie. Give my regards to Gar." And she picked up the basket and went back through her gate.

I was about to follow her with the dipper, but first I had my curiosity to satisfy. I asked the beautiful lady, "What does the long word on top of your wagon mean?"

"Oh. That's just a fancy French language word for candy making."

"*Candy?*" asked Jem. "Was that what was in the basket? No wonder that old lady ran away so fast. She wanted to keep it safe!"

"No," Amalie said with a laugh, "it wasn't candy. Aunt Zilphey doesn't care for nougat and taffy and marzipan. I brought her chicken and other things. It embarrasses and upsets her when I do, but I think it's my duty to her. She doesn't want me to see how she has to live now. Gar says it's terrible for her, but she won't go anyplace else." Now the lady reached under the seat again and brought out a little red-and-white-striped paper bag. She motioned to Jem. "You may have this, little boy. It's a small sample of what we make in our kitchens on Peachtree Street."

Candy? She was giving Jem *candy*. My mouth watered. Poor Southern folk like us hadn't seen candy made out of sugar for months and months. When you could buy it, it cost so much, it might have been gold dust. Honey, and sometimes molasses, were the only sweets we had.

Jem was good about sharing the candy. He brought the bag around to each of us. My piece was a bit of nougat that melted far too fast in my mouth.

Mama said to Amalie, "Thank you. I take it sugar's easy to get here in Atlanta now?"

"Yes, finally. It costs a lot of money, but it's worth it. The Yankee Navy doesn't stop sugar coming in from the West Indies anymore, the way it did during the war. Lots of Atlanta ladies are baking cakes and pies and cookies for the Yankees to buy these days. It's something ladies can do. I didn't think when I started making candy that it'd turn out to be so good for Gar and me. Mostly he drives our wagon—this one we just bought. I drove today, and because of that, I got to meet you all. Isn't that nice, though?"

I watched her eyes glide to Davey, who asked her, "Then there's money to be made doin' things for the Yankees here other than buildin'?"

"That's right, Corporal. Selling to the Yankees is just about the only way to get a little bit rich these days. Do you aim to get rich yourself?"

"You bet I do. Though it goes aginst my grain to get that way off any bluebellies. If I help build here in Atlanta, it'll be for the South, not for the Yankees. They won't be here forever. They can't be! They've got things to do up north."

Miz Amalie had real pretty dimples, along with everything else pretty. She said with a smile, "Then we have to make money off them as fast as ever we can, don't we? I want you to meet my brother. Come to our store, Red-

mond's Confectioners, and meet him. Anybody here can
tell you where it is. All he wants to see is the last of the
bluecoats, too. I'd best be getting back to him now or he'll
fret over my being late. He doesn't like my driving about
alone." As she gathered up the reins, she asked, "Where'll
you be staying in Atlanta?"

Mama told her, "Zilphey said we'd best go to the north
of town till we can get settled in someplace else."

The lady's face clouded up. "If she means that camp for
refugee people, and I think she does, it's not so good a
place. But then you won't be there long. You'll need
money to get in—and money to get you out of it, too.
Good luck to all of you."

After a glance at Davey she chirped to the gray horse,
and off they went at a fast trot. As I went back with the
dipper, I wondered at the lady's last words to us—"Not so
good a place." I hadn't liked them at all.

CHAPTER FOUR

A Real Bad Place

SO MR. TUCKER TURNED THE MULES AROUND once more, and back we went down Edgewood Avenue to Peachtree Street. It wasn't as busy as before because daylight was ending and folks were going home for the night.

How sore my feet were! They were swelling in the heat. I wanted to shuck my shoes off but knew Mama wouldn't allow it.

When I set eyes on the camp where homeless folks like us had to live, I felt like bawling out loud. I wasn't a maw-mouth, but all the same that's how I felt. We'd passed it coming in, and the looks of it hadn't pleased me. And we were to live here! It was a real bad place set along both sides of the road that led back home to Roswell. It was lots worse than our little rented house there. That place had had some trees and Pap's rosebush and our own well, but here there wasn't one single tree, bush, or well at all. A pump sat dead in the middle of a piece of ground that was just red dust blowing in the sunset breeze. There weren't any real houses, either. Everywhere I looked, I saw huts and shanties made out of old lumber taken from other houses. Most of them had tin roofs held down at the edges by rocks so they wouldn't blow off in a high wind. They had doors, all right, but most didn't have any glass in their windows.

Bad as it was, this place was alive with people—men walking about in Confederate uniforms like Davey, women and girls in ragged calico, and barefoot kids running through the dust chasing one another and hollering. It didn't seem that anybody was inside the shanty he or she lived in, and who could blame a body?

As Will Tucker pulled up his team, a tall, skinny woman in a braided straw hat came up to us. She asked Tucker, "Are you lookin' to rent a place here?" Then she spat out a gob of tobacco juice at the mules' front hooves, making them jump.

He shook his head, then pointed to Mama. "The widow Reed's lookin' for one. Not me."

I heard Mama's voice. It sounded strange—like she was trying to get hold of herself. I guessed how she must feel about this camp. She said, "That's right. We'll be needin' a place for a spell till my son here who's a carpenter can build us a house."

The tobacco-chewing woman asked, "How many of you is there?"

Davey answered her, "Six of us."

"Then you'll want two rooms. I got a tent for rent, but

seein' as how you's got a baby, you'll need a house. I got one with two rooms. I'll let you have it for twelve dollars a month, and that's cheap here in Atlanta."

"Twelve dollars?" Mama gasped as she said the words.

"You heard me. There ain't no other place to go less'n you sleep in that wagon."

Old Marilly spoke up. "I've got that much money."

Her twenty-dollar gold piece! I hated to have her spend so much of it all at once.

Mama spoke to Davey and me. "Go with this lady and look the place over to see if it's fittin' for people." She asked the woman, "What happened to the folks who lived in it before? Were they sick? Did they pass over from the sickness?"

"They wasn't ever sick. The fam'ly in it did good earnin' money, and they moved out to a place jest built. They was kin to me, so they left me this house so I could rent it. It's new built—just last January. Come on, I'll show it to you."

Davey and I followed her deeper into the camp, which didn't smell any better than it looked. She stopped at a shanty that looked like all the others. As she threw open the door so we could go inside, I saw a plain dirt floor, two little rooms, six windows with no glass to them, and that was all. There wasn't even a cook stove.

I asked, "How do folks cook here?"

"The weather's good now that it's summertime. They make campfires outside. Most folks here are pleasant enough. They'll share their fire with you if you ask 'em. Did you fetch a skillet and coffeepot with you?"

"Yes'm, we surely did—mattresses, too, and some furnishings." What a strange thing to ask us. She'd seen how loaded Mr. Tucker's wagon was.

She nodded. "Them things is all you'll be needin' for a spell." She called out now, sticking her head out the front door. "Come over here, Sissa Barrows, and meet some new folks. I seen you peekin' out from the side of your house jest now."

Sissa turned out to be a yellow-haired girl between Jem's age and mine, and as dirty a one as I'd ever seen. She limped over but stood a distance away, stubbing her bare big toe into the dust and gawking at us.

Davey told me softly, "We better take this shack, Hannalee. It won't be for long. You stay here and talk to that girl while I go tell Will to unload the wagon."

After he left, the tall woman turned to the girl and asked, "How do you like it here, Sissa?"

The girl chuckled. "Narcissa is what my ma calls me. I like it fine. I don't have to go to school anymore, since the bluebellies came."

I asked, "Are you from here—from Atlanta?"

"I was borned here and lived here all my life. Our house got burned down in the second fire Atlanta had. There was three fires, you know."

"I didn't know there was a whole three of 'em."

"Uh-huh. The second started when our Confederate

Gen'ral Hood began blowin' up the railroad cars. Number one was the one the Yankee firebombs set; and the last one, number three, the great big one, was the one Gen'ral Sherman set on purpose. My pa never came home from the war. Ma thinks he must have got hisself killed and nobody saw it happen, or else he ran way to the West to git out of the army. Some men did that. We didn't have no house after the second fire and no money, so we are where we are now. After the fires kindly folks from as far away as Missouri sent meat and other things for Atlanta folk to eat. Ma works. She'll be back here pretty soon. How many of you are there?"

As I told her I thought of how much better off we were than Narcissa. Though we were poor, there were more of us.

Narcissa went on like she was glad to talk to somebody. "Oh, but that's a lot of folks! My dog, Beauregard, ran away when the Yankees shot their cannons off for such a long time. We never did find him agin. He went wild. Ma thinks he joined up with a bunch of other dogs that went wild and got shot down when folks started comin' back to Atlanta after Gen'ral Sherman left." She sighed. "I miss my dog. We had him a long time. Have you got a dog or a cat with you?"

"Not anymore. We used to have a cat. When she died, we didn't get another one 'cause we doted so much on her."

Narcissa nodded. My, how her hair needed a good

combing and brushing. "That's how it is with poor critters, huh?" She added, "Ma would be honored, I bet, to have you cook your supper with us at her cook fire. She makes one every night."

I said, "I think my mama would be honored, too. My name's Hannalee Reed. That was my big brother, Davey, who left just now."

The skinny woman had been leaning against the shanty listening. Now she asked me, "Are you gonna take the house or not?" She looked cross because I'd spent so much time talking to Sissa.

I said, "My brother says we are. We can pay the rent."

She grunted and started away after Davey, leaving me with Sissa, who had cheered me up some. Zilphey Sanders and the beautiful Amalie hadn't. Us Reeds had had to come to the worst place known in Atlanta to find true niceness. I'd heard Pap say many a time that sometimes poor people who didn't have one other single thing to give could still give kindliness to each other. Miz Amalie hadn't been exactly bad to us, but it was clear to me that she took more interest in Davey than in the rest of us.

All of us helped Mr. Tucker unload his wagon, taking things out and toting them into the shack. We knew he wanted to get back home to Roswell as soon as possible. Deep in my heart I wished we were going back there with him, going home.

By the time we were all unloaded and I'd fetched in the

bag of cornmeal and the slab of bacon that had gotten greasy in the hot sun, Narcissa's ma showed up. Miz Barrows was a thin little lady with her daughter's yellow hair. For all that she wasn't rosy-cheeked and strong-looking, she was lively. She shook hands with each and every one of us and admired Paulina.

When Sissa told her we hoped to share her cook fire, she patted her daughter on the head and came out with, "That's bein' mannerly, Sissa, like I taught you. I'd have been here sooner, but the Yankee lady kept me on for a spell hemmin' linen napkins for her daughter's hope chest." She nodded. "I'm a seamstress, you see."

Mama told her, "We was mill hands in Roswell."

Miz Barrows laughed. "You spin it and weave it and I sew it up, huh? Some of my kin a long time back used to be mill folk in New Manchester. They—"

She would have gone on, but just then Will Tucker came out of our shanty, took off his hat to the ladies, and said, "Miz Reed, Miz Sanders, I'll be on my way back to Roswell now."

Before Mama and Marilly could thank him and say how good he'd been not to ask for any money to move us, Miz Barrows busted out with, "Oh, no! You better not go out on the road tonight. There's been highwaymen about robbin' folks."

Davey asked, "Don't the Yankees stop that?"

"They try to, but they don't seem to."

Mr. Tucker smiled down at the little Atlanta woman. "There ain't much a robber'd get from me. I'll take my chances and go. I only got about a dollar in good money on me. I told my wife I'd be home before day-peep. Good-bye and good luck to all of you."

Davey and Jem shook his hand, and off he went to his waiting mules. Davey turned to Miz Barrows and asked, "Who are the road robbers?"

She shook her head. "They could be lots of men—Yankee deserters, or our own deserters, or men who used to be in the army and can't make no other livin' now than by robbin'."

He asked next, "What folks do they rob?"

Fires were being lit all around us now, and I could see by their light how fierce and eaglelike Davey's thin face looked. Like me, he hoped she'd answer, "Bluebelly Yankees."

She didn't, though. She said, "The newspaper here says they rob us Southern folk jest as readily as they do the Yankees that got gold in their pockets."

I told Jem, "They sure ain't Robin Hoods, then."

Narcissa giggled. She knew who Robin Hood was, too.

We cooked our bacon and baked skillet corn bread side by side with the Barrowses, who were eating the same thing. I figured most of the suppers being cooked here at the fires were just like ours. Later on, when Davey was earning money, we'd have beans and rice and real sugar for our coffee.

After we ate, Miz Barrows told us what it'd been like living in Atlanta during the war. The townfolk lived under martial law, she said. They had to have written passes to travel around, and they couldn't go out at certain hours. Plus they couldn't get stuff like coffee and tea and cloth for love or money.

It was Jem who asked, "Why did our Gen'ral Hood leave Atlanta?"

Miz Barrows let out a deep sigh. "He took the notion into his head to march out and go to Tennessee and win the war there. He didn't, though. He lost two big battles."

I couldn't help but say, "Jem and me saw one of 'em, at Franklin. It was a terrible sight."

The woman's eyes bugged out so you scarcely believed it. "You did, you little shirttail kids? You saw a real battle?"

Jem said proudly, "Yes'm, when we was on our way home from the North."

"Why, it beats believin', it does."

Aunt Marilly said, "Don't let's talk about battles. We done enough of that." She asked Miz Barrows, "Did Hood's leavin' make you grieve?"

"Grieve? In our hearts we were weepin' and wailin', but we didn't let on. Sissa and me went to Peachtree Street and watched our men march out, leavin' Atlanta. They'd fought around Atlanta, but there wasn't any holdin' all 'em Yankees who shelled us day and night."

I asked, "How did it happen that Gen'ral Hood set fire to your house? I bet he didn't do it on purpose." Even as

I said this, in my mind was the memory of how our soldiers had destroyed a bridge last year in Roswell so the Yankees couldn't cross over on it.

"It wasn't on purpose, honey—it was by accident. As I told you, him and almost all his army marched out. It was the second day of September, but he left some men behind to blow up a big lot of railroad cars full of ammunition. They wanted to keep the cars and the ammunition out of the hands of the bluebellies. The cars went up in one big blastin' after another in the middle of the night. Not a blessed soul slept in Atlanta after that. I was workin' all night long as a nurse in the army hospital, so it didn't keep me awake. Sparks from the burnin' railroad cars floated all over. First the sparks set fire to our old shed, and then they spread to our house. They—"

Sissa interrupted her ma. "A neighbor carried me out of our house jest before it crashed down, burnin'. Look at what the fire done to me!"

She lifted her skirt up to her knee now and showed us the big wicked-looking burn scar on the side of her left leg. That burn must have hurt something awful at the time it happened.

With tears in her eyes her mama said, "Sissa was lucky not to get burned alive. There's orphan children here that kindly folks have took in after their pa and ma got burned to death in all the fires Atlanta had."

Jem asked Sissa, "Did it pain you bad?"

Sissa told him, "It don't hurt no more, but it did like fury then. Now all it does is look bad and make my leg a mite stiff."

Mama said, "Burn scars do that. You're a brave girl, Sissa. Did you go to a doctor?"

Miz Barrows answered for her, "She surely did, and he done for her what he could."

Sissa let her skirt fall. I could see she didn't want to talk anymore about her leg. She said, "All that shellin' the bluebellies did burned down other folk's houses, too. Did your town get shot into by cannons, too?"

"No," Mama said softly. "The Union Army jest came ridin' in one July day last year. A couple days later they burned down the house we rented."

Miz Barrows nodded. "We didn't have no money. Nobody did. We traded things. You was lucky not to be here durin' our bombardment days. We lived in holes in the ground."

I said, "We saw one today. What was it like when the Yankees came marchin' in?"

"Strange. Like I couldn't believe it was happenin'. They wasn't no Confederate soldiers here left to surrender Atlanta to the Yankees, so our mayor rode out north of town with a white flag and give up our city to the first Yankee officer he ran into. Before dark there was bluecoats all over the place, with their wagons rollin' down Marietta Street." Miz Barrows shook her head. I could see tears shining on her cheeks now as she said, "To do 'em justice, they didn't harm us none. Their gen'rals said the soldiers wasn't to have any whiskey, and that they had to behave theirselves. They took over some buildin's as headquarters and settled in. They're still camped in huts around the city hall and courthouse grounds."

Davey put the question, "When did old Gen'ral Sherman come in—right away at the head of his troops?"

"No, he didn't. He rode in days later, and he come in strange-like. He could have had a parade and brass bands, but instead he come ridin' in quiet, like he wasn't no hero to the North at all. I didn't even know he was here till Sissa told me. She seen him that very day."

Narcissa was excited to have all of our eyes on her. "I seen Sherman! He's got red hair and a sour face. I was standin' with some boys and girls a-watchin' him and some other officers when I heard one Yankee soldier say to another, 'That's old Cump Sherman, the redheaded one. So he's finally got himself here.' After that some Atlanta boys standin' with us started in on whistlin' 'The Bonny Blue Flag' and 'Dixie,' like they did when the Yankees first come marchin' down Marietta Street. Gen'ral Sherman didn't even look at them. He jest got off his horse and went inside the Neal House, a big one the Yankees took over."

Sissa turned to Jem with a frown on her face. "Don't you ever sing or whistle them songs here now where Yankee soldiers can hear you, though. They put folks in jail for jest about anythin' they want to these days."

Her mother nodded. "Sissa is tellin' you true. They don't have to have any real proof, either, to arrest you. If they want you, they grab you. That's part of what martial law is, I reckon. Folks talk a lot about it nowadays."

Mama said, "We was careful in Roswell, and we will be here, too, won't we, Davey?" I saw how her eyes warned him.

He said flatly, "All I aim to do to the Yankees here is make money off of 'em." He added bitterly, "I guess I can whistle 'Lorena' if I want, though—not that I do."

Miz Barrows said, "I reckon that's safe enough. It's jest a love song."

I reckoned Davey was thinking of his lost love when he said he wouldn't be whistling any love songs. To get his mind off Rosellen, I asked Miz Barrows, "Did you see Sherman leave here in November?"

"We surely did see his soldiers go out to start on their march to Savannah. There was thousands of bluecoats. The men was all singin' 'Glory Hallelujah.' The sun blazed so bright on their muskets, it like to dazzled a person. Sherman hisself left later on—before day-peep one morning. God in heaven! He left men behind to set fire to what little was left of Atlanta. They—"

Sissa busted in with, "Ma, you didn't tell about Sherman sendin' us all away before he burned down our town."

"I was comin' to that, Sissa. He gave out an order for Atlanta people to get ready to leave the town for a place south of here called Rough and Ready. He dumped us in a spot where our Confederates could help us. He didn't aim to burn us up, too. Sissa and me didn't go there, though. We stayed with some kin of mine for a spell, then we came back here when the war ended. Bones of dead horses and mules was everywhere. Froze to death in the winter, they did. Some friends of my husband built us this place. I found work sewin', and we been here ever since."

She wiped her eyes with her apron. "We're waitin' for Zeb, but he ain't been heard of since he went with Cobb's Legion to Manassas. A officer come to see us after the battle there in '62, and said Zeb couldn't be found nowhere."

"That happens," said Davey. "Where there's swamps and rivers to fall into, it happens. I'm sorry to hear about it."

Mama said softly, "I ain't got a husband to wait for. I miss mine sorely." Then she changed the subject. "How do the Yankees treat you here?"

"They don't like us, but they don't hit or cuss us. They ain't so friendly, but we ain't, neither. They do talk strange, though."

This made me nod, thinking of the Yankees I'd lived with in Kentucky and Indiana. The Yankee lady in Kentucky had been a true booger, but Miz Burton, the one in Cannelton, Indiana, was a good soul and kindly to me.

Miz Barrows broke in on my thoughts with, "You all better get to the Yankee provost marshal's office tomorrow and get papers to show that you belong here in Atlanta."

"We know that. We will," promised Mama.

Davey asked, "Do you know anybody who needs a carpenter that can start right away?"

Miz Barrows raised her hands and even laughed. "The whole city's yellin' for 'em and for masons. You'll find work right off. And take Jem and your sister and Sissa with you, too. Since there ain't no schools here now, they may be able to find a job, too. The young-uns can work chippin' mortar off bricks from houses that got blown up or burned. Old bricks got uses here in new houses."

Mama asked, "Will the children be safe?"

"Sure they will—by day. The Yankees keep order pretty good in the city then. They're all over the place like big blue eyesores. Yankees are pourin' their money into Atlanta, and some Southern folk are gettin' rich already." She laughed again. "I bet you didn't know it, but all the money that Atlanta had in its treasury when Gen'ral Sherman rode out of here was one dollar and sixty-four cents. Jest think on that, will you!"

CHAPTER FIVE

"Not Fast Enough by a Long Shot!"

AFTER A BREAKFAST OF CORN BREAD AND LEFTOVER bacon, I went to Sissa's shanty and knocked on the sagging door. She told me from the doorway, "Ma ain't up yet. She fetched home a petticoat that needed new lace and a new drawstring, so she worked real late. I'm ready to go now, and I know where to go, too—to a man Pa used to know from the railroad yard. Even though the Yankees are settin' up the railroad agin, he's buildin' houses these days."

Davey was ready to go get a pass for himself from the provost marshal's office. He had his carpenter's box on a leather sling over his shoulder. He'd shaved his face and brushed his hair and clothes to look his best, and I was proud of him.

He told us at the door of our house, "You kids ain't old enuf yet to need any papers from the Yankees. Ma and Marilly can go later on today."

I was glad that I wouldn't have to go see any Yankees. They made me tremble just passing them on the streets.

Sissa tugged at my hand, so we headed south and then

walked along Peachtree Street. Jem asked, "Where're the peach trees, Sissa? Did the bluebellies burn 'em down?"

She laughed. "This street got named for a real old-time pitch tree—mebbe a turpentine one—but not peaches. Come on. Now we go this way."

She led us all to where a building was rising up. What kind of building, I couldn't tell, because it was only upright boards. Three men were working on it, sawing and hammering. One was big and bald, wearing parts of a Confederate uniform. The second one was a skinny black man in tattered overalls, and the third one was small with longish yellow hair.

"Mr. Dalton," Sissa called out to the bald man.

He slipped his hammer into his back pocket, stepped out of the house, and said, "If it ain't little Narcissa Barrows. How's your mama? Any word of your pa yet?"

"Ma's fine." Then her face fell. "We ain't heard about Pa—not yet we haven't."

"Well, mebbe you will later on."

She pointed to Davey. "I fetched you a carpenter. The rest of us come to clean bricks. We'll do it for a half penny a brick."

Mr. Dalton looked Davey over hard, like he was measuring him. He said, "All right, I'll give you a try workin' for me. What outfit was you in?"

"The Roswell Guards," Davey replied with pride. "I was a carpenter in the cloth mill there."

"House carpenterin' could be diff'rent. We work mighty fast here." His eyes were fixed on Davey's left side and missing hand.

Davey told him, "I'll come back and start workin' soon as I get a pass from the bluebellies here."

Dalton grunted. "Yep, you got to have that. The Yankees come by now and then to look at my men's. I hate to have to take the time to do it."

Davey left in a hurry, and Mr. Dalton waved a big hand at us kids, saying, "Go down the street a piece and ask old Williams to set you to work on his brick pile. I ain't got no bricks right now."

I hugged Sissa for what she was doing for us Reeds, and off Jem and I went with her. We soon found gray-bearded Mr. Williams, who was working on a brick building. He sat us down with little hammers and metal files. We were supposed to knock the old gray mortar from loose bricks he'd piled up. Once we'd gotten a brick clean, we set it in a trough of water to soak off the dirt.

The work was worse than being a bobbin girl in the mill, because there I'd only had to carry a box of bobbins to the looms. Here the bricks were heavy, and they scratched my hands. But the work, though slow, wasn't hard, and I was in good company with Jem and a new friend.

I counted bricks to keep in practice. I'd done forty bricks, Jem fifty-two, and Sissa thirty when I looked up to see Davey standing in the street with riders and carriages passing by behind him. He had his carpentering tools over his shoulder again. The look on his face was so dark, I knew right off something was bad wrong. I dropped my brick, got up, ran to him, and asked, "What's the matter, Davey?"

Between his teeth he told me, "I ain't fast enuf by a long shot to suit Dalton. He says nobody'll hire me as a carpenter here." His voice was bitter. "Sure, one hand can swing a hammer, but it takes two to hold a nail or a board or saw wood. I ain't goin' to be able to follow my trade here like I wanted to."

I cried out, "Oh, Davey!"

He said, cold as ice, "Go on cleanin' bricks, you and Jem. I can't even do that with jest one hand. I'm goin' to where a man can get some whiskey."

I said, "We'll all go back to Mama."

"No, we won't, neither," he yelled at me. "I told you what to do to earn money, and you and Jem do it, Hannalee." And he was gone, walking fast down the street.

Jem and I stuck it out till noontime. When we got paid for our brick cleaning, we lit out for our shanty home. As I figured, Davey wasn't there.

I hated seeing Mama's face as I told her about Davey and the man he'd worked for for only a couple of hours. Her face closed up and went hard. Then she said, "I was afeared he was too hopeful about carpenterin'."

Jem cried out, "I could hold the nails and the boards for him!"

"So could I," I told her.

"No, you're shirttail kids. They wouldn't hire you to help put up a buildin'. And Davey wouldn't let you help him, anyway. No, he's just got to find hisself some other kind of work—and soon, too. You don't know where he went to?"

"No, he told us to stay put. He said he was goin' where he could find some whiskey. Here, Mama." I gave her the pennies I'd earned. So did Jem.

"Thank you, my dears. Sissa, will you watch our shack for us while Miz Sanders and I go to see the Yankees and git our passes? Hannalee, you and Jem and me will take turns carryin' Paulina."

So back we went down the dirt road into Atlanta until we came to the big wide-porch house the Yankees were using as their headquarters. We'd spotted it when we'd first come into the city, and Sissa had told me what the Yankees used it for. Not far away from it we could see neat rows of soldiers' huts on the grounds around the two-story brick city hall. The Yankee flag flew over it, and over this wide-porch house, too. The house had red, white, and blue bunting all along its front, to boot.

A bluebelly soldier with a musket at his shoulder on the porch asked us our business. When Mama told him, he turned us over to another soldier, who led us inside.

I heard the second Yankee laugh as he told a third one passing by us down the dim hallway, "This time it's a whole family of goober grabbers to get in line."

I knew what that meant—peanut-eating Georgia folks—and I didn't like the name. I wanted to say straight out, "That's right, you bluebelly!" But I didn't dare. I could tell by the stiffness of Mama's body that she'd heard it, too.

We waited behind other folks, and finally we got to the front of the line. Mama told a shoulder-straps officer at a table where we were living in Atlanta. He gave Mama and Aunt Marilly pieces of paper to carry with them, and told them always to be ready to show them to any Yankee soldier who asked to see them. Then he said that we could go.

Once we were out on the street again, Mama stopped and took Paulina from me. She said, "I wish I knew where Miz Barrows works. I wish we knew some other folks here besides her who might help us find Davey before he gets hisself into trouble."

"We do," said Aunt Marilly. "We know Zilphey, but she wouldn't be any use to us for that."

Mama told us all, "I reckon we'd best go back to the camp and wait for him to come home when he has a mind to. But I would like to know where he is, at least."

I was just about to turn around and go with her when all at once a word on a gold sign across the street caught my eye—CONFECTIONERS. I pointed to it. "Mama, that's the candy store over there, the one that red-haired lady owns. Mebbe she can help us."

"Mebbe she can. There's no harm in askin' her."

I told Mama, "I think she's sort of taken with Davey."

Aunt Marilly nodded. "I wasn't so concerned with Zil-phey that I didn't take note of that myself."

Jem said, "Anyhow, she won't call us goober grabbers. She's a Confederate from Georgia, too."

So down off the boardwalk we went, dodging passing carriages and wagons in a zigzag to the red-and-white-painted front door of Redmond's Confectioners.

I surely hoped Miz Amalie was there and in the fancy to hand out some more samples. What I'd had yesterday had only honed my taster for more. I hadn't had anything half so good since I'd run away from the nice Yankee lady's house up in Indiana. Miz Burton had been a pudding maker, not a candy maker, though. I just wished there were more Yankees like her, but if there were, I hadn't run into any in Georgia. They seemed dead set on watching us to see our men didn't start up the war again. They knew mountain fighting could go on for years and years.

There was the usual little bell that rang when a person stepped inside a store. I looked up and saw it over the door, shining bright and coppery. While Mama and Jem and Aunt Marilly crowded around me inside, I had a good look around. The shop was clean as a new-whittled whis-tle. It looked new-built to me. There was a sawdust-covered wood floor, a fancy counter covered with glitter-ing jars of hard candy, and on each side, glass-front cases with trays of cow's-cream-color nougat, white marzipan, and tan taffy in them.

Miz Amalie, all dolled up in a pale green gown with white collar and cuffs and a white apron, was behind the counter weighing out candy on a little set of copper scales. As we came in she was putting the candy in a striped bag to give to her customer. He was the one thing about her shop I didn't like. He was a tall Yankee shoulder-straps. Maybe some ladies would say he was handsome, with his dark hair and mustache and dark blue eyes and blue coat to match them, but I didn't see him as anything else but a cussed bluebelly.

Miz Amalie gave us Reeds a quick glance, then she looked away. She smiled up at the Yankee and said, "You said you desired a dollar's worth of horehound lozenges, Captain Hartford?"

"That's right, Miss Redmond, lozenges. They're not for me. They're for Major Fenton. He's got a cold. You know the major."

"Yessiree, I surely do know him. Generally he comes here for nougat."

The captain, who'd only given us one look over his shoulder, said, "Will you be coming to the regimental ball next week, Miss Redmond? If so, will you save me a dance?"

She smiled again as she took his money and gave him the bag. "Oh, I don't know, sir. My work keeps me very busy. Perhaps I shall. I've been asked. Do tell Major Fenton that we Redmonds hope he'll soon be fit as a fiddle again. If he doesn't get well soon, come back and I'll give

you my granny's recipe for a chest plaster that never fails.
Good-bye, Captain."

I figured he might have stayed around longer if we
hadn't come in. He gave us a look that said "goober
grabbers," tipped his hat to Miz Amalie, and went out
with his candy.

I asked her now, "Do you remember us, the Reeds from
Roswell you met at Miz Zilphey Sanders's yesterday?"

"Of course I recall you. I just met you." Then she asked
me, "Where's your big brother, honey?"

Jem answered before thinking on it. "In a saloon somewheres. That's where he said he was goin'." I regretted his
saying this the minute it had popped out of him.

Now she spoke to Mama over Jem's head. "You seem
troubled. What's wrong?"

I knew Mama wouldn't want to tell her why Davey had
gone off to drink. It would be a shameful thing to say.
What would she tell her?

Mama was quiet for a spell, then she said, "Sometimes
my boy's arm pains him, and the only thing that gives him
ease is whiskey. The pain'll pass off in time. We jest came
to Atlanta. We don't know where the menfolk go to
drink. We need Davey to help us unload a wagon." When
Mama sets out to tell a lie, she does a fine job. This was
only a white one, though.

Miz Amalie asked, "Do you want me to get somebody
to go hunt up Corporal Reed? Is that it?"

"That's it," said Mama. "That's exactly it. Find him and fetch him back to us at the camp on the north end of town."

The lady nodded. "I think I can do that. Just wait here a minute." And she went behind the red-and-white-striped curtains into the back of the shop.

We waited a spell, and when she came back, she was with a man. He was as handsome in a red-headed way for a man as she was for a lady. His hair was more of an auburn than hers, and his eyes were dark brown, but you could tell he was close kin to her.

She said, "This is my brother, Garson. He's been unloading sugar barrels for our cooks. He says he'll go find your son, Miz Reed."

I stared at Mr. Redmond. Although he was in his shirt sleeves, he was wearing a fawn- and gold-colored vest. As I watched, he grinned at me, pulled down his sleeves, and buttoned them. When he came out from behind the counter, I could see his fawn-colored trousers and shiny boots. He sure didn't look like any poor Confederate I'd ever seen.

Jem asked, "Was you in Cobb's Legion, too, like a lot of Atlanta menfolk was?"

He laughed. "Who's askin' me?"

"Me, Jem Reed, that's who."

"Jem!" scolded Mama.

Now the man reached down below the counter to get an elegant brown frock coat and a brown slouch hat. Then he told Jem, "I was in our army, boy. Don't you have a worry over that. My sister says I'll know your brother because he's lost part of his left arm."

I said, "He's still got on his uniform. It's part butternut brown and part gray. His first name's Davey."

Mama added, "He's got black hair."

Redmond's eyes took in my hair, Jem's, and Mama's, then he nodded and said, "One arm, black hair, still in uniform. That ought to be enough for me to recognize him in any barroom."

Miz Amalie put in now, "He's good to look at, Gar."

Redmond turned to her. "Isn't there ever enough in the way of admirers for you, Sister? You know what I think about those damn Yankees hanging around in here!"

She flared at him. "They don't hang around. They buy candy. That's more than your fine Southern friends do. *They* just hang around. This is my city, too. I was here when they shelled and burned it."

"Fare-thee-well, dear sister," Gar said with a deep bow. Turning to Mama, he asked, "Where am I to deliver this Davey of yours?"

When Mama told him, he shook his head. "Living out there is enough to drive a man to drink. Don't you worry. I'll find him. There isn't a drinking place in this city that I don't know."

Miz Amalie's pretty face was pouting as she watched her brother go out the door. She sighed and told us, "You might as well go on home. What Gar says is true. If any man in Atlanta can find your son, Miz Reed, it'll be my brother. He knows all the saloons for sure."

Mama said, "Thank you kindly. We're sorry to have troubled you. It's good of you to help us when you don't even know us."

The lady brightened some. "Why shouldn't I? We're all caught together in this mess of trouble, aren't we? These sugar barrels can get unloaded just as well by somebody else I hire for an hour on the street as by my brother. For certain, he won't be back here before dark. Don't be surprised if he brings your son back pretty late."

After hearing that we left the shop. I was glad that somebody was out looking for Davey, but Jem had one complaint. "She didn't give us anythin' this time."

"You hush, Jem," came from Mama. "We ain't beggars. It's plenty that she's doin' for us."

That didn't shut him up, though. As we went along in the afternoon heat and dust, he went on talking. "Davey's full growed. He can find his own way home from saloons when he has a mind to come back."

Mama turned on him. "That ain't why I want him found and fetched home. Don't I know he's a man now, and that he's seen a sight of mis'ry? It's his temper I'm thinkin' about. I don't want him to get full of whiskey to the point that he picks a fight with somebody and gets hisself hurt. Worse yet, he could get in trouble with the

Yankees. You know how hot a temper he's got and how mule-headed he can be."

I nodded at what Mama had said. I knew very well how set in his ways Davey could be. That was how he'd lost Rosellen last summer.

Aunt Marilly said now, "All I want is to get back to my mattress, fetch a cool drink of water, and lay down. Walkin' about Atlanta in this heat ain't my idea of how a body my age ought to spend her time."

Mama put on her Indian queen look, stood straight as she could, and said, "Someday, Marilly, we won't walk at all! We'll ride in carriages the way rich folk do. You jest wait and see. Be hopeful. Come on, Jem. Walk beside Hannalee. Don't lag behind. That ain't the Reed way. When Davey gets home, we'll talk things over and make up our minds what we're goin' to do tomorrow."

Just as she finished talking, a bunch of Yankee horse soldiers rode past. Everybody moved to the side of the road so they could trot down the middle. Their black horses kicked up plenty of dust. Jem sneezed, but not me. I held my nose and glared at the bluebellies.

As I took my fingers off my nose and sucked in a deep breath of clear air, I told myself that I wasn't finding it one bit easy to be hopeful for us in Atlanta. What could a man with only one hand, a man who couldn't do more than write his own name, do that would put eats on the table and get us into a real house?

CHAPTER SIX

"Hannibal Sanders"?

IT WAS JUST BEFORE SUNSET WHEN MR. RED-
mond fetched Davey home to us. My big brother
wasn't hanging on to him or being led, so he couldn't have
had too much to drink. Nobody had a hard word for
Davey; we understood his reasons. Mama had told us that
we weren't supposed to mention carpentering to him anymore. As I looked at him sitting on a stool outside our
shanty, I noted that he didn't have his box of carpenter's
tools with him. Maybe he'd sold them. It wouldn't be
hard to find a buyer in Atlanta.

After thanking him for what he'd done, Mama
asked Gar Redmond to stay and drink some coffee with
us.

"No, Miz Reed, I'd best be on my way."

"Well, then, come back anytime to visit us."

I could tell from the look on his face that this wouldn't
be too likely. Gar didn't cotton to our shacktown. Why
should he?

As the man turned to go, Davey spoke up. "It don't
appear to me that a man has to pay for his own whiskey

here in Atlanta." He laughed and added, "Not when he's been chewed up in the war like me."

Redmond patted Davey on the shoulder. "And he shouldn't have to, either. You come see me at the end of the week and maybe I'll have something going for you. I got an idea that just might do. It could suit you down to the ground!"

"Work for Davey, you mean?" asked Mama.

"That'd be it."

Davey put in, "Before you go, Gar, show my folks what you fetched back from Appomattox with you. They'd like to see it, too."

"Sure, Davey." Gar Redmond reached into his fine coat and brought out a little book bound in purple velvet. He said, "It's only a little thing, so you'll have to come close to see it."

Sissa Barrows, who'd stood by listening all this time, crowded among us Reeds to look, too. All I saw was a dirty piece of blue, red, and gold cloth.

I asked, "What is it, Mr. Redmond?"

The man explained. "A piece of the flag that my regiment carried all through the war. I was at Appomattox with my outfit when General Lee surrendered. The damn Yankees expected us to give up our battle flags to them. Although some fools did, a couple of regiments burned theirs rather than lay them on the ground with their weapons. My colonel cut ours up with scissors so every man jack got a piece of it for his own to remember the war by."

Aunt Marilly exclaimed, "Well, I never heard of anythin' half so smart as that! At first I thought it was jest a quilt scrap."

"No, it's silk, pure silk. My sister helped sew it when the war started."

Mama asked, "Was you Redmonds allus candy makers?"

"No. Pa and I bought cotton and shipped it by rail to the North and West. The war put an end to cotton shipping."

I asked, "Is your house still standin'?"

"No." His jaw muscles tightened. "Cump Sherman burned it down along with a whole row of good houses. It was almost new, too. Pa's health wasn't good when the war began. He went down to Rough and Ready when Sherman threw out the townfolk, got pneumonia in the rain, and died."

"And your ma?" Mama asked gently.

"She passed on when Amalie was just a year old."

"So there's jest you and your sister, huh?"

"That's it." He nodded. "As I told Davey here, Pa had buried money, gold, before the Yankees entered Atlanta. He told Amalie where it was. The bluebellies never knew about it, or they would have grabbed it the way they grabbed everything else. Amalie waited till I got home from the war, then we dug it up. We used some of it to build a store with a place to live behind it and went into the candy business." He spoke bitterly. "A lot of folks—Yankees, mostly—have a sweet tooth, and after the war sugar could be gotten hold of again."

Aunt Marilly sighed. "I never thought I'd say I got weary of molasses-flavor, but I did, and even that was hard to find at the end, too."

Redmond laughed. "You can forget molasses now—and honey, too."

Hearing Gar talk about the war and his losses made me decide I took to him. I said, "Mr. Redmond, you and your sister are sure mighty good to us when you hardly know us."

He had a wide smile. "You're good Southerners. The Atlanta that's building now won't be like the one Amalie and I grew up in. Atlanta will belong to everybody who helps build her. Towns like Charleston and Savannah and New Orleans—and I've seen them all—they're not like Atlanta. They're old and set in their ways. Atlanta moves with the times." He spoke just to Davey now. "Remember, come see me. Come to the shop. I may not be there because I have business in a lot of places, but Amalie'll most likely know where to find me. If she doesn't, just wait and let her stuff you with bonbons. She's good at that when her fancy lights on a person."

I liked listening to Gar. The Redmonds were fancy folk,

and quality, who'd always lived better than we had and sure talked finer than us mill hands. But all the same, they were mighty pleasant to us.

After Gar left, Davey said quietly, "He said he saw Gen'ral Lee cry after he had to give up to the bluebelly army. He told me what Lee had said to his men there. Gar knew the words by heart and made me say them back to him." Davey's voice got deeper. " 'Boys, I have done the best I could for you. Go home now, and if you make as good citizens as you have soldiers, you will do well, and I shall always be proud of you. Good-bye, and God bless you all.' "

Nobody said one single word. Tears came to my eyes. Then Jem said, "I wished I could have been there. If I'd seen Lee's horse, Traveller, I'd have patted his neck and mebbe given him a lump of sugar—if I had one in my pocket."

Mama put an end to our sad talk about the war by saying, "It's time for you and me to be startin' supper, Hannalee. Miz Barrows said she'd fetch us a chicken already plucked so we could fry it up tonight."

I looked quickly at Davey, who was sitting still, thinking. On what? I wondered.

I walked over to Mama. She was bent over feeding the fire with twigs and straw to get it started. Leaning down, I told her, "Jem and me can go back and clean more bricks tomorrow. The man who hired us said he could use us all week. There's a big heap of bricks that still needs workin' on."

Mama nodded, then said very quietly, "Paulina's near to weaned by now. Marilly can stay here and tend to her. There ought to be work here for somebody like me."

"But, Mama, I never did see one cloth mill hereabouts, or ever heard tell of one!"

"No matter, there must be other kinds of work I can do. Hannalee, we won't go to the Freedman's Bureau to ask for food. That ain't the Reed way, and Davey'd hate it. The way I see it, the faster we get out of this camp, the better. And the fastest way to do that is for all of us to work who can. Davey'll find somethin' that he can do, but we oughtn't to depend on him if we hope to get ahead here. It's goin' to take all of us."

"Yes, mebbe so, Mama."

What difference did it make if all of us worked? Wasn't that what we'd always done in Roswell in the mill? If the war hadn't come along to change our lives, Paulina would have gone there as a bobbin girl when she got old enough. I looked down at my hands, all scratched and cut from the bricks I'd cleaned today. I'd surely be pleased to get better work than this. Chipping bricks was cussed hard.

But all at once a sad thought came to me. What about the way my head looked? So far as I could see, there wasn't another girl in Atlanta who had hair as short as me. I wasn't about to pretend to be a boy again, the way I'd done up in Indiana, calling myself Hannibal Sanders, but who'd hire me as a girl, looking the way I did? Well, maybe I could find some work that didn't set me out front where folks would have to look at me. I said to Mama, "My not havin' a good head of hair's goin' to cause me trouble gettin' work. I can't wear sunbonnets and hats all the time I work indoors."

She nodded. "That's the truth, honey, but don't fret over it. I've thought on the matter, and somethin' can be done about it."

"Oh, what, Mama?"

"I'll tell you after I done some more workin' out."

"Mama, what does your Cherokee blood say about us now that Davey can't carpenter?"

She gave me a glance from those shining black Indian eyes of hers and said in a whisper, "We got to stick together like mornin' glories stick on a picket fence. Lord help us if we don't. Don't you stop prayin' every night."

"I won't. I'll pray harder'n ever. I'll even . . ."

I would have gone on some, but just then Miz Barrows came into sight lugging a woven straw basket with our chicken in it. Davey got up to take it from her.

I watched Miz Barrows's pale, tired face light up when she saw Davey. For a fact, all womenfolk seemed to dote on him. I figured Jem would grow up to be that way, too. But not me. My brothers had gotten the good looks and the smiling ways, and it wasn't fair.

After our chicken supper Mama and Miz Barrows had a talk a distance away from where the rest of us sat beside the dying fire. I tailed along after them and heard Mama tell Sissa's mother everything that had happened during the day. She finished up with, "I need work, but what kind of work could I get here? I ain't never been anythin' but a mill hand."

Miz Barrows pursed her mouth, then said, "Miz Reed, you took care of a house and your family. That's called housekeepin' here, and housekeepers can be wanted."

I gave a little start of misery. That's what I'd done up in Yankeeland, and I hadn't took to it one bit.

Mama asked her, "How do I go about gettin' to be a housekeeper?"

"Oh, that ain't hard. Read the *Atlanta Intelligencer* where folks put in advertisements about jobs. A lot of Yankee men came down from the North and left their womenfolk behind. Some don't cotton to hotel livin', so they buy or build houses, and then they need a woman to keep it up for 'em. There never was a man I ever saw who doted on housekeepin'."

Mama whispered, "Yankees? I'd be workin' in a Yankee's house all day long?"

Miz Barrows had a laugh like Sissa's. "Well, most likely the Yankee won't be there, and if he's not, what diff'rence will it make to you? You may not have to set eyes on him at all if he goes off to work the way most of 'em do. You'll probably have to cook some, though."

By the firelight I saw Mama's nod. "That's fine by me. I'm a plain cook, but I never heard no complaints over what I set on the table."

I said, "You're a jim-dandy cook, Mama!"

She paid me no heed. She only said, "My girl Hannalee here can read and write some. She can read the newspaper for me tomorrow mornin'. We'll go see whoever wants a housekeeper—Yankee or no Yankee. I don't care."

Miz Barrows said, "That's the spirit, Miz Reed." Now her voice changed. "It's mighty hard on us womenfolk who's lost their men. Sometimes I wished my man didn't feel the need to join up to fight the Yankees. He didn't hold with slavery—said seein' human bein's all chained up and for sale made him sick."

"Neither did Mr. Reed," replied Mama, "and neither does Davey. My menfolk didn't go to war for the Confederacy because they favored slave holdin', but only because they was Southerners and they couldn't abide the idea of anybody sayin' they was slackers. They was carpenters, and carpenters was needed bad in our mill. If they'd wanted to, they could have stayed out of the army. But that ain't the Reed menfolk's way."

"No"—Miz Barrows sighed—"it wasn't my man's way, either. Lordy, but I'd surely like to know what happened to him. A Yankee officer, a Lieutenant Marcus somethin' or other, that I talked to today told me I'd most likely never hear. The Yankee Army has plenty of men missin', too. That lieutenant was visitin' the ladies I sew

for. I think he's sweet on one of the girls. He jest came
here last month with a new batch of horse troops. He hails
from Indiana—from some town on the Ohio River where
they got a big cloth mill. He says one thing he plans on
doin' before he gets discharged and goes back home is to
find a Georgia boy, a boy mill hand by the name of
Hannibal Sanders."

Hannibal Sanders! An icy shiver ran up my spine. Could
this Yankee be hunting for *me*? I'd worked in a Yankee
mill in Indiana under that very name. But what would a
Yankee officer want to find me for? My heart froze in my
chest.

Thank goodness for the dark. Miz Barrows didn't see
my fright. As natural-sounding as I could, I said, "Sanders
is a common name, Miz Barrows. It's Aunt Marilly's, but
I don't think she's kin to any Hannibal Sanders. Did the
bluebelly say what Hannibal looked like? Aunt Marilly
said she had red hair when she was young."

"No, he didn't exactly say. He said the boy was dark-
complected. He'd been a good bobbin boy who'd run
away last year."

I got more shivers. Oh, that fit me all right—every bit
of it. *I was the one for sure!*

I could tell from Mama's voice she was thinking what I
was. I'd told her all about how I'd called myself Hannibal
Sanders. I'd used my real name at first, but when I ran
away from the folks in Louisville, I turned into Hannibal

Sanders. Mama said, calm as could be, "I do believe I once heard tell of a boy who was kin to Marilly down Macon way. He was somewhere between Jem's and Hannalee's ages. I believe she said they named him Hannibal, a strange name to my way of thinkin'. If you see that Yankee officer agin, tell him to ride down to Macon and ask 'round for any Sanderses there."

Miz Barrows gave a little start. "Wait a minute! He said somethin' else, too. He said he was goin' to be ridin' over to Roswell and ask 'round. He said the boy hailed from there. Didn't you all come from there?"

Mama told her, "We did, but there never was no Sanders boy by that name there. We'd best get back to our house now. The bugs are bad out here away from the fires."

Back we went, and after we'd washed our plates and skillets, we went inside to bed.

Before I lay down next to Marilly, Mama called me over to her mattress. She reached under it and fetched out a cloth bag full of things she'd gotten out of our old house before the bluebellies had burned it. She hauled out a pair of shears and her old snood. Women mill hands would stuff their long hair into a snood and wear it over the backs of their heads to keep their hair out of the mill machinery. Many a woman had been hurt bad by being dragged by her hair into the moving parts. Mama hadn't worn her black knitted snood for a long time.

Now she let down her beautiful hair. It was so long, she could sit on it. Hair was a woman's crowning glory, and Mama was so proud of hers. She gave me the shears and ordered, "Cut off some of it, Hannalee."

"No, Mama! *Why?*" It was rippling, black as river water in the night.

"Because I tell you to. Stuff what you cut inside the snood, then tie the snood over your head. My hair color's close enough to yours to fool any Yankee lookin' for a boy. God only knows why he's doin' that."

"Oh, Mama. I don't want to cut your pretty hair," I cried, but I sheared off a third, stuffed it carefully into the snood, and tied its strings into a bow on top of my head while Mama pinned up what was left of her hair into a knot.

"Now jest let that Yankee come lookin' for a mill boy named Hannibal Sanders," said Mama with a smile. "He'll never find him here with us. There's just my two boys, my baby girl, and my beautiful, long-haired daughter, Hannalee."

CHAPTER SEVEN

Some Salvations, I Reckon

To GET USED TO THE FEEL OF THE SNOOD, I WORE IT TIED to my head all night long. It felt mighty strange, I must say. In the morning I smoothed out the hair and retied it. After breakfast I asked Sissa and Miz Barrows how it looked on me.

Sissa said, "It appears natcheral, Hannalee, like you growed it yourself."

Miz Barrows told me, "You're lucky your ma and you got the same color hair."

I couldn't help but say, "Our havin' black hair's the Indian blood comin' out in us. Mama's purty. Black hair does fine by her. And Davey and Jem's got good looks, but I wish I'd turned out to be red-headed like Pap and Paulina. That color becomes a lady more."

Miz Barrows comforted me with, "There's some fine old songs about black bein' the color of a person's true love's hair."

I'd heard them songs, too, but it appeared to me that golden locks like Rosellen's drew love more easy than black ones. Nobody had ever said he loved *me*! Anyhow,

87

I was weary of hair troubles by now. Cutting mine off to try to disguise stubborn Jem as a girl hadn't brought me anything but grief.

I told Miz Barrows, "Me and Mama will be goin' to the *Intelligencer* today to see the paper and find Mama work."

"Good. And the best of luck to you, Hannalee."

Mama and I left the rest of the family home and walked through the busy city to the newspaper office. I thought Mama looked fine in her yellow straw bonnet with the black chicken-feathers trim. We went inside. The office had desks up front, and a printing press machine behind. What a ruction there was in there! The noise was so loud that I had to holler at the man at the front desk.

"I come to see the help-wanted ads."

"That'll cost you a penny to look, little gal."

That wasn't much. I coughed up the penny, took a morning paper from him, and Mama and I went outside onto the boardwalk with it. It wasn't a thick paper. I didn't try to read the news but turned right off to where it said "Help Wanted." Then I ran my fingers down to where I saw the word *housekeeper*. I told Mama, "There's three notices here wantin' housekeepin' ladies. Wait a minute. One of 'em wants a lady to 'live in.' I reckon that means day and night, huh?"

"I can't do that, Hannalee. How about them other two?"

I said, "They don't say that. We got to go to the people themselves and ask, Mama."

The first place we walked to was on Ivy Street, which wasn't too far from where Zilphey Sanders lived. It was a white house behind a low brick wall. It looked fine to us as we went up the walk—not busted up by the war at all.

Mama gently banged the door knocker once. The door was opened by a black girl Jem's age or so. She was wearing a new red calico dress and had a feather duster in her hand. She only looked at me and didn't say a word.

I asked, "Is your mama the housekeeper here?"

"My mama sure is. We started yesterday."

I told her politely, "Thank you," and we turned around and left for Marietta Street, where the other job was. It was quite a tramp, and we were hot and dusty before we got there. Mama and I stopped at a pump and washed our faces and hands. By the time we reached the two-story gray house with a red carriage house out behind, we were both weary. I'd surely done my share of walking in shoes the last three days.

This house was nice, too. There were yellow rambler roses in bloom on a trellis, and white wisteria in the overhang of the deep front veranda. It all smelled mighty sweet.

"Pray, Hannalee," said Mama, and I did.

After Mama pulled on a bell for a long time, we heard footsteps. Finally the door was opened by a little, bent-over, gray-headed man who'd once been tall, judging by the length of his legs. He had on a ruffly white shirt, gray trousers, and a black vest. I thought he looked elegant.

He asked in a deep, Yankee-sounding voice, "Did you come about my housekeeper notice in the paper?"

"Yes, sir," said Mama.

"Well, you look pretty strong to me, madam. Come inside and we'll have ourselves a talk."

He'd called Mama "madam." I guessed that was Yankee talk for "ma'am." I started inside, too, but he barred my way. Without saying a word to me he shut the door. I sat down on the top step of the veranda to wait. While I waited, I thought about the ways of Yankees. I'd sort of expected a glass of buttermilk or cold water or something. Even Southern men who lived alone would have thought to give me something to drink, but I didn't get anything, not even a single word.

I waited and waited, and finally Mama came out. I could tell from the look on her face that she'd gotten the job, but I could also tell something hadn't pleased her much.

As we went down his walk she told me, "I start tomorrow at seven in the mornin' and work till eight at night. He wants to eat at five-thirty. He's willin' to pay me good but, oh, that house of his is a caution, Hannalee! He jest came from Illinois and bought it last week. Soldiers had been livin' in it for a time. They must have bedded down their horses inside. You ought to see the walls and floors I'm goin' to have to scrub."

"Ain't that just like dirty bluebellies, though?"

She gave me a laugh. "It wasn't Yankees who made the mess. It was our own soldiers before they left Atlanta last summer."

"*Our Confederates?*"

She nodded. "Yes. Danged few men are neat by nature, Hannalee. Davey and Jem got trained right by me, but who knows how they'll behave away from home? Anyhow, it's work I can do. Mr. Levy says he ain't got the stomach for real fancy cookin'. He ain't married. He never was. All he wants is a clean house, plain, decent vittles on the table, and his evenings to hisself to read. He's goin' to start up a bookstore here."

A bookstore! That was something to know. "Mama, does he know you can't read?"

"He never asked me."

"Had other women come here after the job, too?"

"Yes, but he said they was too young and flighty for him. He liked my bein' older, and wanted somebody who'd worked hard before. He said he's worked hard all his life."

"Did you tell him about Pap and Davey?"

"Yes, I did. I didn't hold back the truth that we was Confederates. He said he hadn't expected any work-seekin' Yankee ladies to come lookin' for the job. I think he'll be a fair man if I do good work. Him and me should get on together. At least we won't have to go to the Freedman's Bureau and ask for food. We'll earn it."

"Oh, Mama, I'm surely glad to hear that!" I put my hand into hers and was shocked to find out how cold it was. Mama must have been plenty scared in there, though she wouldn't let on to me. I gave her hand a loving squeeze, and she squeezed back.

She added now, "You know what else? He said you was a nice, bright-lookin' girl-child."

Was I ever tickled at this compliment! She went on, "It's the snood that done it. Now what we got to do is get a job for you, Hannalee."

"Tomorrow, Mama. I'll look for a job, too."

The way it turned out, Jem got work before I did. When I got home with Mama, we found both him and Davey gone. Aunt Marilly rocked Paulina in her arms and told us, "Them two headed out not long after you left. They's both huntin' for work."

I asked, "What can Jem do? Chip bricks like Sissa?"

Mama told me quietly, "He could work in the Roswell mills as a lap boy. Mebbe there's work for him here, too— better work than cleanin' old bricks. He ain't allus goin' to dance to your tune, Hannalee."

"Mama, he didn't ever do that!"

"Didn't he? Wasn't you the one that gave the orders to him up in Yankeeland?"

"I had to. I was the oldest one."

"Well, he's a year older now."

It wasn't until dark that my brothers came home. Though Davey was still down at the mouth, Jem was almost prancing. "I got me a job," he called out as we sat by our cook fire. Without our getting a chance to ask what it was, he hollered, "Davey and me went to the newspaper office to see if there was work for him, and while we was there, one of the men there asked me if I wanted to go to work for him."

I couldn't believe my ears. "*You'll* be workin' on a paper, Jem? You can't hardly read yet! Newspapers is all words on paper."

"I don't have to read. All I got to do is go 'round to stores and ask folks if they want to have a ad put in the paper. If they do, they write it out for me, and I take it back to the *Intelligencer*. I don't have to read—only talk. I'll get paid four cents for every ad I git. If I go to the stores, the storekeeper don't have to go hisself, or send somebody to the newspaper."

I couldn't find the words to tell him how lucky he'd been. Mama said, "Now that's fine, Jemmy! I got work housekeepin' today, too." She looked at Davey, who'd hunkered down at the fire. "How about you, son?"

He only grunted and said, "They want men to drive wagons and carpenters and bricklayers. There don't seem to be much a one-handed man can do. Gar said he'd come up with somethin', and I think he will. He's plenty smart. I'll wait on him now." Suddenly Davey turned his face to us and said, "I heard tell from a man from Roswell we met on Peachtree Street a little while ago that Will Tucker had one of his mules shot dead on his way back there the night he fetched us here to Atlanta. Some men stopped him on the road and robbed him."

"Oh, my Lord!" I put my hands at the sides of my face.

"Did he get hurt?" asked Mama.

"No, he's all right. There's some other news, though." Davey took the cup of chicory coffee Miz Barrows handed him, blowed on it, and went on. "The Roswell man said a Yankee officer was there early this mornin' lookin' around for a fam'ly by the name of Sanders. The bluebelly was told there wasn't anybody 'cept for you, Marilly, and that you'd gone to Atlanta. He wasn't lookin' for Rosellen. He wanted a boy Hannalee's age."

I asked, "Did the man from Roswell tell you the Yankee's name?"

Davey shook his head and laughed. "I reckon he didn't tell it 'cause nobody there would ask him."

Though Mama's eyes met mine through the flames, neither of us said anything. That dang Yankee soldier sure wasn't wasting any time looking for me, was he? But why? I hadn't done anything wrong but run away because I was homesick and hated the North. I didn't owe anybody any money. I'd worked hard and paid for everything

I'd got. Besides, the war was over. I wasn't any danger to the Yankees. Oh, this was a mystery and a misery, too!

Though I hunted up and down Atlanta for two days, I didn't find work. I went to the *Intelligencer* with Jem and looked at the ads. But the only jobs were for lady seamstresses and hat trimmers and laundresses, jobs I didn't know how to do.

Late in the afternoon of the third day, I passed by the Beaufort Hotel where bluebelly officers sat in a row of chairs on the veranda. As I tromped by I spotted a sign in the window of the store across from the hotel. It said, GIRL WANTED. *Girl wanted!* That was me!

I stepped off the new-built wooden walk, moved between wagons and carriages, and had half crossed the street when I heard my name called out.

It was Miz Redmond, driving her green wagon. She was prettier than ever in a peach-colored gown. She reined in, leaned down, and told me, "Please tell that handsome brother of yours that my brother'll be coming to see him real soon with some news I think he'll like."

I nodded. "I'll do that very thing, Miz Amalie."

"Good-bye, then." She waved to some of the Yankee soldiers as she drove past. I recognized one of them as the very same captain I'd seen in her candy store. She sure did make a hit with the bluebellies. You could tell by the way they grinned and called out to her and lifted their hats.

As I looked away from the Yankee officers on the veranda, I took note of a thin black girl who was sweeping the front steps of the hotel. She was pretty, wearing a gray dress with a long white apron and a white ruffly edged cap. She took note of my staring and stared back at me. It was clear to me that she'd gotten herself work as a maid in the hotel, though she didn't look much older than I was.

The shop that wanted a girl smelled nice, of new wood. It sold cloth and thread and ribbons and laces. There were big bolts of calico and gingham standing on the floor, and three long counters. On some shelves behind them I saw silks shining bright, as well as satins, wool, and linen. One thing a mill hand knew was cloth.

A broad-shouldered, blue-eyed man with a yellow beard came forward to meet me. "Yes, miss?"

He had a Yankee voice.

I turned around, pointed to his sign, and said, "It says you want a girl."

"Oh, yes." He smiled down at me. Then he asked, "How old are you?"

"Fifteen," I lied. "I used to be a mill worker. I know plenty about cloth."

"I imagine you might. Have you ever sold it, though?"

"No, sir, but I know how to measure it out by the yard. I can read and write some. I can add up prices, too. I been to school." That wasn't quite true. The minister's wife hadn't run a real school.

"Well, that's good to hear. What's your name?"

"Hannalee Reed."

"Where's your family?"

"They live here in Atlanta now—my mama and two brothers and a baby sister."

"Do you want to work here?"

I looked again at the pretty fabrics and fine trimmings and told him, "Yes, sir, I do like cloth."

He smiled, then called out, "Mary Anne, please come here."

I backed away. "You've already got yourself a worker girl? I'll be on my way, then."

"No, no. I'm calling my daughter."

The gray velvet curtains at the rear of the store parted, and out came a girl. She was almost as tall as I was, but much plumper. She had pale gold corkscrew curls, white skin that would sunburn fast, marble-round blue eyes, and pink cheeks. She was dressed in pink to match them.

"I'm Mr. Herrick," the man told me. "This is Mary Anne. We're from Connecticut."

"Hello." Mary Anne held out a small white hand that had a gold ring with a red stone in it on her fourth finger. I took her hand in my brown one and shook it. But shaking hands wasn't something I'd ever learned to do. The Yankee girl pulled free fast from my rough grip, and

I said, "Sorry, ma'am." Turning to Mr. Herrick, I asked, "Am I hired?"

"Yes, you are, Hannalee. Be here Monday morning at eight. You'll work to seven o'clock. I'll pay you fifty cents a day till I see how you do. Does that suit you?"

"It suits me." Then I added, "I better tell you right now. I only got two dresses—this blue one and a red gingham."

He only nodded. "You'll wear a blue-striped apron that'll cover you. It's got pockets in it for scissors and cards of pins."

Mary Anne told me, "You'll wear a yellow tape measure around your neck, too."

"That's all fine with me. I'll be here Monday morning. Good-bye."

Happily I headed for the door and opened it to go out, but Mary Anne walked right out behind me. She came close to me and said, "Oh, I'm so glad you aren't a grown-up! Ladies have been coming here all day long because of the sign Papa put up this morning. I asked him to please hire somebody close to my age—not somebody old."

"Why do that?"

"Because I'm so lonesome here in Atlanta. I don't know anybody at all but Papa. There isn't a school for me to go to. All I can do all day is read my books and embroider samplers back where we live behind the shop. Mama died three years ago. It's just Papa and me now. We came here to get over sad memories. I hope you and I can be friends."

Friends? I could barely believe my ears. After a four-year-long war a Yankee was asking *me* to be a friend!

She went on. "I'm so weary of reading all the time. I need somebody to talk to."

Reading? Books! *Weary of reading books!* I gave her a nod, not a smile. I said, "I reckon we can talk sometimes if you have a mind to and I ain't busy."

Sure I'd talk to her, if it meant I could keep this job. I'd like handling all that handsome cloth that was woven in Yankee and French mills. I'd never dreamed there could be such pretty colors in shining cloth, though. We'd never made such fine stuff in our Roswell mill. It'd be pure pleasure to touch the silks and satins and velvets, too. I reckoned I could put up with the company of this Yankee girl for that.

CHAPTER EIGHT

Atlanta Living

WHEN I GOT BACK TO THE SHANTYTOWN, I WAITED TO tell everyone I'd found work. I wanted Mama to be there to hear it.

When she came, she looked used up from all that cleaning and scrubbing she'd been doing for Mr. Levy. From being a maid in Yankeeland, I knew what hard work housework could be.

As we ate a soup of dried field beans that Marilly had cooked, I proudly told everybody, "I start to work Monday in a place that sells yard goods. The Yankee who hired me's goin' to pay me fifty cents a day."

"That's fair wages for somebody your age," Miz Barrows said.

I blew on my soup and answered, "I'm glad to hear that. The cloth's fine to look at. There's only one thing wrong with the job. It's my boss's girl, Mary Anne."

Mama asked, "What's wrong with her?"

"She wants me to be her friend. How can I be friends with a Yankee girl? And how come she wants to be friends with me, a Confederate? She says she's lonesome here in Atlanta."

Miz Barrows and Sissa came to sit beside me with their supper. The woman said, "She's tellin' you the truth, Hannalee. Atlanta womenfolk work at whatever they can do to make money from the bluebellies because their families need the money. Sellin' things to the Yankees don't mean that Southern women invite 'em inside their houses or make friends with 'em, though. That's askin' too much. I sew for Yankee ladies and answer their questions, but I don't never start a talk between us. They ask me and I answer, but that's all I do."

Davey put in, "What you're sayin' is that 'round the Yankees it's strictly business, huh?"

"That's right. That's all it is." She smiled at me. "There's no call for you to be real friendly-like, Hannalee. That girl don't deserve it."

I nodded and took another mouthful of the watery green soup. "That Mary Anne Herrick should have thought about what we suffered in the war before she asked to get so all-fired friendly with me. She didn't get hurt that I can see, even if she ain't got any ma."

"No ma?" asked Mama quickly.

"No, there's jest her and her pa. But they've got to be rich to own all them silks and satin goods."

Now Aunt Marilly spoke up. "They ain't so rich if there's only the two of 'em." The look on her face told me she was thinking of her lost Rosellen.

That made me turn to Miz Barrows and ask, "Did that

bluebelly officer ever come back—the one that wanted to know about Roswell folks?"

"I haven't seen him since."

By now Jem had finished his bowl of soup. Sitting on his heels, he told us, "I run all over town today, from Five Points all the way out on Marietta Road. I seen Miz Amalie Redmond out there, drivin' her green wagon."

I said, "I saw her today, too. She said her brother'd come to see Davey soon."

Jem asked, "Was that Yankee captain with her?"

"Yankee captain? No, she was alone. He was sittin' on the front porch of the Beaufort Hotel when I seen her."

"Well, she had a Yankee shoulder-straps when I spied her out on Marietta Road. He was drivin' her wagon. He wasn't that Yankee we seen. This one had a yellow mustache. He was a major."

"What Miz Redmond does isn't our business," scolded Mama.

"This ain't any business her brother Gar's gonna like," came from Davey. "Sellin' candy to bluebellies is one thing—ridin' out with 'em's another."

That very night Mr. Redmond showed up at our shanty. He didn't tell us what he was up to or what he wanted. He asked me to fetch Davey, and when I did, off they went through the camp together.

I got the idea that Gar didn't much fancy Mama and Jem

and me—just Davey. Well, there wasn't anything odd about that—menfolk sometimes wanted to be together to talk about things they didn't say to womenfolk. Davey and Pap had been that way. Womenfolk were, too. Look how close Mama and I were!

Davey came home some time in the middle of the night. Worried about him, I slipped out of bed without waking Aunt Marilly and sat down on his and Jem's mattress to help him get his boots off. Getting boots off with one hand was a trick he hadn't mastered yet.

I asked softly, "Did you have a good time, Davey?"

He spoke softly, too. "It ain't what you think. We didn't go to no barrooms. Gar took me to meet some men he knows."

"Atlanta menfolk?"

"That's right, the kind of men who think the way he does."

I had his boots off for him now, and he led me out of the shanty into the moonlight.

"What do you think, Davey?" I asked him out there.

"Nothin' I'd want you to bother your head about." He was quiet for a bit, then he said, "I'll be startin' to work Monday, too. Gar found somethin' for me that he says I can do easy. It only takes one hand."

I was so excited, I almost let out a whoop of joy. "What is it, Davey?"

"Workin' a telegraph key. One hand can do that fine."

"But you don't know how. Did they teach you in the army?"

"No, the soldiers in the signal corps did that. I seen 'em do it, though. They went lickety-split fast on the key, sendin' out messages over the wires. There's a school here where they teach telegraph operators. Gar says he's gonna learn along with me startin' Monday."

Something about what he was telling me was buzzing in my head—something was wrong with it. And then all at once I knew what it was. "But, Davey, you never learned to read and write! How're you goin' to work a telegraph key when you can't do them things?"

He laughed. "Gar and me talked about that. He claims I don't need to. All I got to learn is the letters A to Z, and what dashes and dots stand for each one. The messages I'll be sendin' over the wire will be printed out on paper. I'll just use the key to tap out the letters." He laughed again. "Gar says men in foreign countries send out messages all the time in languages they can't read. Mebbe I'll learn to read by sendin' words."

I shook my head. "I don't know if you can learn that way, but I guess you can send a message without knowin' what you're sendin', at that."

"There's one more thing, Hannalee. It's bad."

"Huh?"

"I won't get paid while I'm learnin'. Gar has to pay to learn, but he talked with the man who runs the school about me, and he's willin' to let me learn for free because I got so bad wounded. There won't be no money comin' in from me for a spell, I reckon."

I sighed. Well, Mama and Jem and I were earning wages, at least.

Davey went on. "Later on I'll earn real good money telegraphin'. Gar says they're hollerin' for telegraph operators out West."

"Out West?" Would Davey leave us so soon?

"Sure, Hannalee. Once I get you and Mama and Jem and the baby and Marilly settled in good here, I might go out to California." He paused. "It ain't as if there's anythin' much to keep me here."

Rosellen! Sure as could be, he was thinking of her—so far away in Indiana.

I told him, "I thought we'd stay together, Davey—all us Reeds."

"Little sister, you don't need me like you think you do."

"Oh, yes, we do! I know you grieve for Rosellen, but look around for another girl. There's lots of purty ones here. Look at Miz Amalie. She favors you, ain't you noticed?"

"I've taken note."

"She'd be honored to have you court her."

"Mebbe so. Mebbe later when I get work telegraphin'. Gar'd like that fine. It'd take her mind off Yankees."

This made me think of the officer who was hunting for me. While we stood together in the night wind I told Davey about my using the name Hannibal Sanders up north after I'd run away to Rosellen in Indiana. I told him the new name had been her idea—to throw Yankee folks who might be looking for me under my true name off my track. I let him know how worried I was that the bluebelly was seeking me so hard, he'd ridden to Roswell.

Davey thought for a while, then said, "He don't stand any chance of findin' you here where you're a Reed and a girl. So Rosellen thought up that name for you to hide under? She cared that much for you. Is that why Mama truly cut off her hair for you? The war's over and done with, Hannalee. What if he does find you? You didn't do anythin' bad up there, did you?"

"Not that I can think of, except for runnin' away two times. I just wonder why he's after Hannibal Sanders, though. I never once set eyes on a Yankee soldier up in Indiana, so he can't know me by sight."

Davey said firmly, "Well, put him out of your mind."

I shivered. It was cold outside. I told him, "Well, I ain't about to march up to the provost marshal here and say I used to be Hannibal Sanders and that I heard your army's lookin' for me and I surrender to you."

Davey laughed. I liked hearing that. He seemed happier now.

I asked, "How come you got back here so late? Didn't

bluebellies stop you for your pass 'cause you were out so late?"

"They did, but Gar was with me. He knows plenty of Yankees. They let him and me go on."

"You surely do dote on Gar."

"He's my friend, Hannalee."

Now four of us Reeds went off somewheres in the mornings. Davey and I went in the same direction for a while, then he turned west while I went east. Miz Barrows walked with me as far as the cloth store, then went to her Yankee lady's house.

Even with everybody but Aunt Marilly and Paulina busy working, we weren't getting ahead as fast as we'd hoped. That was because the prices of our rent and food were so high. We still needed corn bread, beans, peas, and bacon. Mama said Mr. Levy ate better now because she shopped and cooked for him after she cleaned and dusted and polished up his house. She could have taken food home from his kitchen, but she told me she wouldn't think about it for a minute—even if we all went a mite hungry at times. Mr. Levy had told her to make herself something to eat midday, and she did, but she did it sparingly. Mama said the food she ate would gag her if she knew her children needed more than they were getting. As for bringing his food home to us, it would be plain stealing!

What Mama said about being hungry was true enough. At noon we ate only corn bread, something we could carry in our pockets, and we ate every crumb of that, too. So Mary Anne Herrick couldn't see how poor I was, I ate my bread sitting out on her back steps. When I first began to work for her father, she offered me ginger cakes and apple tarts. I was tempted but didn't give in. I thanked her kindly and tried to forget how tasty those things looked. After my refusing two times, she didn't offer me anything more, and she stayed behind the curtains of the store. No Yankee was going to buy my friendship!

One day Jem met Mr. Herrick when he came to the shop trying to get him to advertise in the *Intelligencer*. I thought Jem looked mighty fine and was proud to claim him as my brother. The folks at the newspaper had gotten him a brown jacket that covered his old raggedy shirt, and some new tan trousers that went over his knees. The duds were only loaned to him. He had to leave them at the newspaper office when he quit work at dusk, the same as I left my striped apron on a shelf in the Herricks' store. Jem's hair was slicked down handsome-like, and his smile was wide. I told my Yankee boss, "This here's my brother Jem. He's workin' for the Atlanta newspaper, sellin' ads."

This made Jem frown at me. "I can do my own talkin', Hannalee!" He turned his side to me and started to tell Mr. Herrick about the ads.

Mr. Herrick listened, then said, "Sure, I'll take out an ad. I've got an order of French silk coming in next week. I might as well let all Atlanta know about it before it arrives."

"Then, please, mister, write up the ad the way you want it in the paper. The ad's a dollar."

While Mr. Herrick wrote up the ad Jem came over to loll against my counter. That was the moment Mary Anne picked to come into the store. She had on a fancy pale blue taffeta gown that made her eyes so blue, they almost popped out of her face.

"Hello," she said to Jem.

He gawked at her like he'd never seen a Yankee girl before, let alone such a pretty and plump one. I knew he'd seen them up north last year, but probably not one like her.

He said, "Hello."

Because I had to, I said, "This is my brother Jem."

"I know. I heard you talking from behind the curtains where I was reading. It's awful dull back there all day long." She looked him up and down and added, "You look hot, Jem. I'll bet running around in all that heat and dust makes you thirsty. Wouldn't you like a glass of lemonade? It's all made and ready."

"I surely would like some."

"Well, then, I'll bring you a glass."

Oh, Jem, I thought! Out she went between the curtains,

and was right back with a glass of lemonade for him. He drank it down quickly, said, "Thank you," and handed the glass back to her.

Mary Anne smiled at me and went behind the curtains once more. She hadn't ever offered me any lemonade.

I whispered to Jem, "You shouldn't have done that. That's bein' nice to bluebellies!"

"Well, she was nice to me."

"Ain't it enuf that they won the war? We don't need to be friendly with 'em, too. She knows better than to offer me her old lemonade. I've told her no to cookies and tarts."

He grinned. "I had a thirst, Hannalee." Then he clumped over to where Mr. Herrick was holding out the piece of paper he'd written the ad on.

When Jem left, my boss said to me, "Your brother's a manly little fellow."

I said, "Jem's all right. My big brother Davey's a Confederate hero, though. He lost part of his arm last year. He's trainin' to be a telegraph operator."

Mr. Herrick looked troubled. "There isn't a lot a one-armed man can do to make a living."

"No, there ain't. He can't even lay out cloth, or cut and fold it—do girl's work like me."

"Well, Hannalee, if there's anything I can do for him . . ."

"There ain't, Mr. Herrick. Us Reeds will do fine. We

stick together. Now that Pap's dead and Davey's one-armed, we stick together closer than ever."

"Yes, that's the way good families ought to be. I wish there'd never been a war at all."

"So do I, sir." I dared to ask, "Were you in it?"

"No, my wife was sick for years on end. I had to buy a substitute to go in my place. I was never a soldier."

I couldn't help but say, "Davey and Pap didn't do that. They wouldn't—even if they could afford to pay someone to go in the army for 'em. Anyhow, us Confederates didn't allow substitutes."

"Oh, yes, you did, Hannalee."

Now, that was a big surprise to me. Hearing this made me bite down hard on my lower lip. That wasn't right at all. I'd thought only Yankees did that. I didn't choose to think this was true of our army, too, but if Mr. Herrick said so, it probably was. I reckoned he wouldn't tell me this just to make me feel bad. I kept my head down while I ran my hands along the bolt of satin cloth in front of me. It was purple-red—magenta, "the Queen of Colors," he'd told me. Two Yankee ladies had bought lengths of it today. When I'd cut it for them, I'd been thinking how fine black-haired Mama would look in this color. It wouldn't suit those pale Yankee ladies at all.

Mama! I sighed a little. She was worried, and so was I. New as it was, the wind and dust blew through the cracks and walls of the shanty we rented and, of course, whatever wanted to came in through the glassless windows. The man who'd built it hadn't cared one bit about what it would be like to live in it in wintertime. By hook or by crook, come November we'd have to be in a better place. We couldn't live there through the winter! With Aunt Marilly as old as she was, and Paulina so little, we would need a tighter house. Miz Barrows was worried, too, about what she and Sissa would do in cold weather. She and Mama talked about it a lot around the cook fire at night.

Our second week in Atlanta, the heat stopped and dark clouds came in from the north, where all our sour luck seemed to come from over the last four years. It commenced to rain and didn't stop for three days. We had to put pots and pans on the dirt floor of our shanty to catch the drips.

The rain turned the dusty streets into mud a person had to slog through or use stepping-stones to cross over. The stepping-stones weren't big enough for two people to walk on at the same time, so mostly ladies in hoopskirts and Yankee soldiers used them. Being smart, I went to work barefoot, washed my feet on the back porch of the store, and then put on my shoes and stockings. Since I left after Mama, she never knew I went around shoeless in the city.

On the fourth day the sun came out again, and so did

everybody's laundry. That day Mr. Herrick sent me across
the street with a parcel of lace for a lady living in the
Beaufort Hotel. I waited for my chance on the stones and
skipped over, not once looking toward the Yankee officers sitting on the porch. They were always there off-
duty, gawking and grinning.

I'd never been inside a hotel before. This one was all
red plush, gold paint, and fancy kerosene lamps. Atlanta
had had gaslights on the streets before General Sherman
came, but he'd busted them up, too, and the gasworks.
There was a dining room to the right of the big room
where more officers sat in elegant chairs, and on the left
was a barroom saloon. Men were standing around the
bar with one boot on the brass rail, talking and drinking
and spitting tobacco juice into cuspidors. It was hazy
with cigar smoke in there. Some of the men wore
Union Army blue; others were dressed in ordinary
clothes. I reckoned they were Yankee businessmen like
Mr. Levy and Mr. Herrick, or maybe even what Davey
said Gar called "scalawags," Southern men who had
friendly dealings with the Yankees. Gar called Northern
men who'd come down to pick the carcass of the South
"carpetbaggers" because they carried all they owned in
bags made out of carpet cloth.

A whiskery man behind a big desk called me over and
asked, "What can I do for you, my girl?"

After I'd taken note of his nice black broadcloth coat

and white vest, I told him, "Not a thing. I jest fetched this here for a lady."

He frowned down at the name on the package and said, "Yes, I see. We have a lady guest here by that name. I'll see that she gets the parcel. You don't have to take it upstairs to her." He gave me a sharp look. "Go down the hallway to your left and leave by the side door at the rear. You need not go back through the lobby and front door again."

I knew what he meant. He didn't approve of my striped apron and old shoes. Well, I didn't think too highly of him, either. He had a Georgia accent, and he was only working for the Yankees, the same way I was.

I asked, "What part of Georgia is you from, mister?"

He gave me a cold look and, like I figured, didn't answer me.

I did what he ordered, going down the long, dark hall to the end and out into the sunshine at the back of the hotel.

CHAPTER NINE

Delie

WHAT I SAW THERE MADE ME GASP—CLOTHESLINES, more clotheslines than I'd ever seen before in my whole life, and on them white sheets and pillowcases and towels swaying in the breeze. Moving around in all that drying linen was the pretty black girl I'd spotted a while back sweeping the hotel steps. She was walking about in the mud under the lines barefoot, saving her shoe leather, too.

While I stood there enjoying the sight of all that clean cloth blowing in the wind, something bad happened. Three little boys, all younger than Jem, came skidding around the corner of the hotel. Two had yellow hair and looked alike. The third was red-headed. The minute they got close to the laundry, they stooped, filled their fists with mud, and let it fly at the closest sheets. Plop! Plop went the brown mud on the white cloth.

The black girl gave a yell. "Git 'way, you devil boys!" and ran at them. I ran, too, and while she collared one of the tow-headed boys I got the redhead. Oh, what a shaking I gave him! Nothing riles a female more than dirt thrown on clean, drying laundry. The third boy took to his heels.

The black girl and I let go of our culprits at about the same time. I'd taken note that she wasn't whaling hers like he deserved, just holding him and giving him a shake now and then.

When those two had run off, hooting, she turned to me and said, "I thank you for what you done for me."

I told her, "What they did was mighty wicked. I'd whale the tar out of my little brother if he was bad like them three."

She nodded and went over to the muddied sheets. I followed and helped her take the dirty sheets down so they could be washed again.

I told her, "My name's Hannalee Reed. I work across the way at the yard-goods store."

She was shy. "I seen you go to work. I start work a mite earlier than you do."

"Do you live here at the hotel?"

She nodded her head. "I do, but my mama lives in a camp at the south end of town."

I said, "I live in one at the north end."

She was quiet for a moment, then said, "My name's Delie."

"Why, that's my mama's name! Do you have any more fam'ly?"

"Yes, besides my mama I got a sister."

"I've got a sister, but she's only a baby yet."

"Mine's older'n I am."

Suddenly a window closed at the back of the hotel and Delie looked up, grabbed the basket of linens by its handles, and headed for another rear door. As she left, she called out, "Yes, Miz Cassie! I'm comin'. Comin' fast!"

She was going back to work. I'd best get back, too. Bosses hated tarrying on the job. Mill work had taught me that much.

As I went around the side of the hotel to the front and crossed the street again, I thought of Delic. Where had she come from? Had she lived in Atlanta all along? Had her family's place been destroyed like most of the other folks here? There was something about her that I took to. She hadn't wept and wailed over what the rascally boys had done. She'd acted just the way I had—sailed right into them, got hold of one, and took care of him. Maybe they'd bedeviled her before? Boys in a gang could do that to a girl. I'd seen it before. It was a kind of teasing, but it hurt all the same. They weren't Yankees. I could tell from their accents as they yelled back at Delie and me as we shook them. They were Georgia boys.

When I got back to the cloth store, Mr. Herrick asked me, "Did you deliver the parcel, Hannalee?"

"Yes, sir, I did. I'm a mite late 'cause I had to go out and 'round the back way, and once I was there I had to stop some boys from throwin' mud on the hotel laundry."

He let out his breath. "I've noticed that there are quite a number of boys running wild up and down the streets.

They're like packs of dogs. They ought to be in school."

"Yes, sir, they ought to be." How I wished I was, too.

"How well do you read, Hannalee?" he asked me all at once.

"Not so good."

"Would you like to borrow a book from my daughter?"

"No, sir. I think it'd be too hard for me." I'd had a gander at some of Mary Anne's when I went into the Herrick parlor on errands. They were big books with big words in them.

"What if I got you an easy book, a book of stories?"

"Stories?" I bit my lips. *Easy* stories! I thought of the ginger cakes and tarts I'd turned down—but stories? Those other things had been food for the stomach—once ate up, they were gone. Stories would feed me over and over. I couldn't help but tell him, "Why, yes, sir, I'd like that. You can take what it costs out of my wages—if it don't cost too much."

He smiled. "How about a book of fairy tales?"

Fairy tales? I'd never read any of those. Our preacher's wife in Roswell had told me about Cinderella, but to read about her for myself! "I reckon I'd like fairy tales."

"Then that's what it will be. You may read here when there aren't any customers. It's a good way to pass the time."

"Oh, yes, sir, it truly is."

Before I realized it, I was giving a Yankee a smile.

And then, out of the blue, in came Amalie Redmond, looking like a princess in a storybook. She was all in green-and-white sprigged muslin with a big straw hat with green ribbons. A Yankee officer was with her, but not the one I'd seen in the candy store, or the one with a yellow mustache Jem had seen driving her wagon. This one was tall and lanky with brown hair and blue eyes. Because he wore high black boots and had crossed sabers on his collar, I could tell he was a bluebelly cavalryman. Those were the kind of horse soldiers who'd carried Jem and me off last summer. I'd never in my life forget Yankee cavalry uniforms!

Miz Amalie saw me right off and cried out, "Here you are! Davey said you were working here, Hannalee."

"Yes'm. What can I do for you?"

"I need two blue plumes for a bonnet, and ten yards of sky-blue satin from that new shipment, if you have it."

Mr. Herrick came over to help her choose the feathers and the shade of blue she'd like. That left her Yankee standing there. He came over to me and leaned on my counter.

He said, "I hear from Miss Redmond that your family hails from Roswell."

I froze like a frog in a heavy frost. Was this *the* Yankee who was looking for Hannibal Sanders?

I told him, "Yes, sir, we come from Roswell."

He asked, "Did you ever know a boy named Hannibal Sanders there?"

It was *him*! I shook my head. I couldn't speak. Finally I got out, "What's he done that the Union Army's lookin' for him?"

He laughed. "He was a bad boy."

A bad boy? I asked, "Where'd you get to know him?"

"I never actually knew him. I heard about him, though. I know a great deal about that boy."

I couldn't ask him any more. I felt sick to my stomach with fright. I was going to be sick. I clapped my hands over my mouth and ran to the privy behind the store where I threw up over and over again.

When I finally stopped, I leaned against the side of the privy, getting my strength back. I was so glad Mama had thought to give me her snood and hair.

When I came back to the shop, Miz Amalie and the officer were gone. Mr. Herrick and Mary Anne were looking at me worried-like, so I told them, "I'll be all right now. Somethin' I ate must have been bad for me. Did Miz Redmond buy her satin?"

"No," Mary Anne said. "She couldn't find the right color of blue to suit her. She's going to a military ball with that officer. Wasn't he handsome, though?" She was misty-eyed. "He told me he was from Indiana, and that he's sorry you got sick."

Indiana? It all went together. That's where I'd worked as Hannibal Sanders, all right.

★   ★   ★

Of course, the minute Mama got home, I told her about the Yankee lieutenant. She said, "Amalie Redmond told him we was from Roswell? Well, don't worry, Hannalee. He wouldn't ever guess you were Hannibal, so you're safe enuf. What'd he say Hannibal did?"

"He said that he'd been bad."

"Was you?"

"No. I worked in the mill with Rosellen and helped that Miz Burton with the chores because her husband and boys were in the Yankee Army. She helped me with my schoolin' and fed me good, too. You wouldn't believe there'd be so much goodness in Yankees like her. The only bad thing I done was to run away from her. But other mill workers who got sent north have come back home now, and the Yankees don't care about them."

"Don't fret yourself. He figgers you can't be Hannibal. . . ."

At that very moment Davey came in with Jem, who'd taken to hanging around the telegraph school when he was done at the newspaper. I told Davey about the Yankee shoulder-straps and Amalie. He only grinned and said, "She sure does cut a swath through the blue-bellies. Yep, she must have said we was from Roswell. Gar don't talk with Yankees the way she does. Forgit about the officer. He'll soon give up huntin' what never was a true person. Nobody knows the name you used but us—and . . ."

"And Rosellen." I finished what Davey was about to say. He didn't like to say her name.

Suddenly he busted out with, "And she don't care about us no more! If she had, she could have wrote a letter by now askin' how you all are. Just 'cause she thinks I got killed in the war, that don't mean she shouldn't care about the rest of us Reeds. And what about Marilly, her own kin? Can't she write and ask after her health?" He took off his cap and threw it against the wall.

"Davey, she can't read or write."

"She could get somebody up there to write for her."

Mama put in softly, "Davey, we wanted a letter from you, too."

He gave her a glare. "What—ask a Yankee in that hospital to write for me? I wouldn't do that if I was dyin' and gaspin' out my last breath." He said next, "I won't be here for supper. Gar and me're goin' to be busy tonight. I won't be back till late. All I have time to do is change my shirt and shave."

I knew from the temper he was in not to cross him, so I kept quiet.

The month of June went by, and July, too, with us three Reeds working and saving every penny we could in an old worn-out sock of Jem's. It didn't appear to me that we saved a lot, though. It cost plenty just to feed us and buy soap and other things we had to have to stay alive and clean. Prices didn't come down one bit. I fetched Mama the cheapest brown calico Mr. Herrick had, to make her some new aprons, me a new dress, and a shirt for Jem so we wouldn't be in rags. Davey had to be outfitted all the way in a new coat and shirt and trousers because he didn't have one rag but his old uniform, and you saw less and less of those on the Atlanta streets all the time. Come September he was due to start drawing wages.

He was out a lot during the nights now, going wherever he went with Gar Redmond. Sometimes Gar came with a buggy, but generally with two horses. Davey would meet him outside our camp, since Gar didn't like coming inside to fetch him. Davey bought himself a pocket watch so he'd be on time, and that cost a pretty penny.

For a fact, Davey worried Mama. She'd stand at the door of our shanty and stare after him when he left. Once I heard Miz Barrows say the word *Regulators,* like it was a question. Her voice sounded proud as she said it.

Mama turned to her and said sharply, "Not my Davey! He's got some good sense, Sally."

I hadn't known what Regulators were, so I asked Mama later.

She told me, sounding glum, "They're Southern men who don't take to what's goin' on today. They're still tryin' to fight the war however they can."

"How can they do that?"

"By beatin' up on black folks they think are actin' like they was important. By settin' fires in places."

"Then they don't fight the Yankees?"

"Not right out, they don't. The Yankees want to catch 'em, and if they do, they can hang 'em. Their martial law's mighty quick."

Well, this sure gave me something to think about. I asked, "Were the men who robbed old Mr. Tucker and killed his mule Regulators?"

"No, I don't think so. They was jest plain robbers. They could even have been Yankee deserters scared to go back home. It ain't one bit safe to travel out of Atlanta at night. Mr. Levy told me that he's bought property, cotton land, twenty miles southwest of here, and he has to hire hisself guards with pistols and rifles to take him to see it."

Hearing of the Regulators made me think of that black girl, Delie, and wonder how she was getting on. I'd like to see her, but would she welcome me?

The next morning I walked to work, and as luck had it, I ran into Delie on the street in front of the hotel. I had my book under my arm, as I was always reading about fairies and giants and grim goblins.

She stopped a few feet away and said, "You got yourself a book!"

I said, "You bet. It's a present to me from the Yankee man I work for. He ain't a bad sort."

"He gave you a gift?"

"He surely did. I'm learnin' from it to read better."

"You can read purty good, huh?"

"No, I have to ask for help on big words."

She nodded. "I'm tryin' to teach myself to read. When I do washin', I put the alphabet up on top of my washboard. When I scrub, I look at the letters. I can't do words yet at all."

I said, "What you're doin' is right. The alphabet comes first."

"Did you have somebody teach you in a real school?"

"No, I was a mill hand in Roswell before we come down here. The preacher's wife there taught me some, and another lady up north, but now I go on by my lonesome."

Delie traced an O in the dust with her foot. She said, "That's a O. I was a slave. I worked in a big house as a house slave before I was set free by Abe Lincoln and we all come here to Atlanta. Slaves wasn't ever taught to read and to write. My mama and my grandma say that when there's a school here for us blacks, they'll both come to it. So will everybody else—no matter how old."

I said, "You sure do set a store on learnin'. Well, so do I. I could teach you what I know. I can come at noontime and mebbe sit on the back stoop of the hotel with you."

"I'm not sure. I seen you once with your brother, and I could tell he was a Confederate soldier. I don't like soldiers. I'll think on it, though."

"What's your last name, Delie?"

"Brackett. It was the name the folks had where we was all slaves. They owned us. They didn't treat us too bad. Mama picked that name. Pa's dead."

"So's my pap. He died of camp fever in the war."

"Mine got lockjaw before the war from workin' in the master's stable."

I nodded. I knew how a person got that awful sickness—from a puncture wound he or she got in places where there were horses.

At that instant the bells chimed in the steeple of one of the churches, the Catholic one, for eight o'clock. It had bells now. It had been the only church in Atlanta where the pastor stayed on while the city was being shot at by Yankee cannons.

Delie and I both jumped at the clanging, and off we ran to work. As she left, Delie waved and I waved back.

I hoped she'd meet me the next day to say it was fine for us to get together at noon.

But, as it turned out, that never happened. After our first meeting I only saw her at a distance, sweeping the porch or washing hotel windows. Whenever she spotted me, she'd wave, but that was all. I reckoned maybe she didn't want to be friends with me any more than I wanted to be with Mary Anne Herrick.

To tell the truth, I was sort of lonesome here in Atlanta, lonesome for girl company my own age. In Roswell I was friendly with the other girl mill hands near my age, and with Rosellen, who big-sistered me at times. Sissa was younger'n me—too much younger. It appeared to me that here in Atlanta I had one girl my age I didn't want to be closer to because she was a Yankee who didn't know what hard work and suffering in wartime was about. Then I had another one who did know, but because she was black and I was white, she most likely didn't want to get any closer to me than she already was. I'd have a lot more to talk about with Delie Brackett than with Mary Anne Herrick. While she sat behind her velvet curtains and read, I lugged around bolts of cloth to suit her pa's orders. She couldn't even cook, but I baked corn bread when Mama was late and fried bacon and sometimes cooked a chicken I'd bought. Mary Anne and her pa ate every meal, even breakfast, at the hotel across the street.

I couldn't hate the Yankee girl who wanted to be nice to me. How could I when she was friendly? But somehow I felt years and years older than she was—though she was a half year older than me. Sometimes I was so full of pent-up feelings that I felt like busting out and crying in front of her and her pa, but I didn't. They wouldn't understand.

I couldn't truly hate these Yankees. As I saw it, our life in Atlanta was going along better than I'd hoped when I'd been so worried in Roswell. If only we could save more money faster! I guess I just had to stay hopeful about that.

CHAPTER TEN

Caught!

I N THE MIDDLE OF THE NIGHT I WOKE UP AND SAT STRAIGHT up on my mattress, gasping for breath. I remembered something that I'd put out of my mind for nearly a year. I'd stolen a pencil from Miz Burton's house! It was the one I'd used to write Rosellen that Davey was dead. It was all gone, because I'd used it up writing words I knew on wooden boards.

Was that cussed bluebelly shoulder-straps after me because of a *pencil*? Why, it couldn't have been worth more than two cents. Those Indiana Yankees must be a mean, vengeful bunch. I only took the pencil as a token of the kind Yankee lady. I'd hoped at the time she wouldn't think I was a thief, but it appeared to me this was just what she did think.

I sorely wished I could hunt up that Yankee lieutenant, hand him two cents, and tell him to leave Hannibal Sanders be. But if I did, he'd know for sure that I knew the whereabouts of Hannibal. Oh, but this was pure cussedness! Never again would I ever take anything that wasn't mine, not even a sprig of honeysuckle from a front porch.

There just wasn't any telling which way a Yankee would jump.

I didn't close my eyes a wink the rest of that night, so I was weary as I walked to the store the next morning. The rain, coming down in buckets, didn't help my mood any. As always, I looked across the way to see if I could spy out Delie, and I did. Seeing the work she was doing, I sure felt sorry for her. She was on her hands and knees polishing a row of six brass spittoons. There wasn't any nastier job than emptying out all that brown tobacco spit and old cigar stubs. Just thinking about it made my insides start to churn.

I wanted to wave at Delie, but she had her back to me, so I went on to the cloth store. Because of the book he'd given me, I was feeling a mite more friendly to Mr. Herrick these days. This morning I had a question to ask him, one that had been bedeviling me for a while. I'd been waiting to ask it when Mary Anne wasn't around, and since I heard noises from overhead as I came up to him, I reckoned she was just getting up.

Mr. Herrick was winding royal-blue ribbon onto a big spool, and I said, "Can I ask you somethin'?"

"Ask on, Hannalee."

"How come you hired me to work here when your girl could do my work jest as good as I can?"

He gave me a sharp look, then a smile. "You're pretty sharp, aren't you? You're right, of course. There is a reason. I've come down from the North and gone into business here. I need to have Southern ladies as well as the wives of Northern soldiers come to buy fabrics from me. So I wanted a Georgian to work here to make the Georgia ladies feel comfortable. Look around you, Hannalee. You'll find that many Northerners here have taken on Southern partners for the same reason."

I said, "I didn't know that. I don't know that many folks here yet. Miz Redmond, who was jest in here, don't have a Yankee partner."

He laughed. "Miss Redmond doesn't need one. She's got just about every Union Army soldier here eating out of her hand, as well as eating her candy."

I nodded. "I guess that's so. I've noticed that the only cloth the Atlanta ladies can afford to buy is calico and gingham. They don't never buy any nice lace."

"That will change in time, Hannalee. Atlanta is going to change very swiftly."

I wanted to say that I didn't think Southern folk's feelings about losing the war would change so fast as he thought, but I held my tongue. It appeared to me that a lot of getting by in hard times had to do with tongue-holding. It didn't come all that natural to me or any of the rest of us proud Roswell Reeds.

As Mr. Herrick finished winding the ribbon I asked him, "Do you want me to show Mary Anne to do what I do?"

"Why not, Hannalee, and I do wish you would let her

help you with your reading. You don't have to sit out
alone on the back steps every day, you know. She'd sit
with you if you asked her to, and she'd like to give you
something more to eat than corn bread."

So he knew what I ate? I couldn't meet his eyes, so I
looked at the cracked toes of my shoes. I ought to be mad
at the Herricks because they had spied on me, but they
meant well. It was getting danged hard to hate them—
they were treating me so tenderly. Pap would have said
they were killing me with kindness, or at least killing my
hate.

I told him, "I don't mind bein' by myself out there, but
I'll think on what you said jest now. I promise you I will."

When I got home that night, I told Mama why Mr.
Herrick had wanted a Georgia girl working for him.

She nodded her head and told me, "I've took note of
that already, Hannalee. Mr. Levy's takin' on a partner, a
man who come here last week from Virginia. I bet it's for
the same reason—so Southern folk can't be so hot against
'em as they'd like to be." Then she changed the subject. "I
hope Davey comes home to supper tonight. He wasn't
here last night or the night before."

I said, "Don't fret over him. He's puttin' on some flesh
eatin' somewheres. Haven't you seen that?"

"I have, and you know I rejoice, but I'd like to know
where he goes nighttimes."

"He's most likely with Mr. Redmond."

"I reckon so, but where does Mr. Redmond go?"

"I'd like to know that, too," came from Marilly. "Mebbe it's dances and theaters and drinkin' saloons, too."

Mama sighed. "But mebbe it's more than that, Marilly. Mr. Levy told me that there's men ridin' around outside the city at night, masked and wearin' long duster coats that cover 'em from neck to heels. Some of 'em rob folks on the road like Will Tucker got robbed, but others thrash and whip any black women and men they get their hands on. The Yankee soldiers are on the lookout for them night riders."

Jem hadn't said a word, but now he put in, "Davey ain't got a horse—if that's what you're thinkin', Ma."

"Horses can be borrowed, Jem."

I asked Mama, "Wouldn't Davey find it hard to ride a horse when he's only got one hand?"

"I dunno. I heard tell that our Gen'ral Hood was one-armed and so bad shot up by the war's end that he had to be lifted onto his horse and tied there. But all the same, he was ridin'. Davey's got two good strong legs under him." She turned to me as she took cornmeal from the cloth sack. "Do you two see your brother with other menfolk besides Redmond?"

I told her, "Twice I seen Davey go into the Beaufort Hotel with Gar, but not with anybody else."

Jem volunteered, "I seen him with two other men once comin' out of his telegraph school. They was his age and was wearin' parts of Confederate uniforms the way he used to. Davey saw me across the street, but by the time I could get over to him past a big old wagon in the way, he was gone, and they was, too."

"Mr. Redmond wasn't with 'em, Jem?"

"No, Ma, not that time."

"Oh, I'm just hopeful that Davey will learn telegraphin' real good so that when he ends his trainin', he'll be paid enuf for us to find work that we'd all like doin' better."

I said quickly, "I like my work all right, Mama."

"I like mine, too," Jem told her.

"Well, housekeepin' ain't my first choice. Cleanin' my own house is all right. Somebody else's don't suit me so well."

"Hatin' to do housework is why I ran away up in Louisville, Kentucky, last year to go to Rosellen in Indiana and do mill work."

"Rosellen." Marilly said the name very softly. "I wonder if I'll see my dyin' day before I set eyes on her or have word of her agin?"

I told her, "I'm sorry I brought up her name. I didn't mean to. It jest sprang out of my mouth."

Aunt Marilla covered my hand with hers as I sat beside her on our mattress. "It don't matter, Hannalee. She ain't never far from the thoughts of any one of us."

"Do you think Davey's turnin' sweet on Miz Amalie?" Jem asked.

"I dunno," I said. "It'd mebbe do him good if he was, and she got sweet on him. I see her in her wagon plenty of times through my store window. That Yankee shoulder-straps we saw in the candy store rides alongside her a lot on his horse. There's another Yankee, a yellow-mustached one, on her other side plenty often, too. Mebbe he's the one who likes horehound lozenges. Both of 'em live at the Beaufort Hotel."

Aunt Marilly came out with, "There's too many bees buzzin' around that Amalie flower. One thing I can say for my Rosellen is that she was constant when it came to Davey Reed. There never was another one for her since the time she was ten years old."

Nobody added to what Marilly said, but I guessed what we were all thinking. There never had been another girl in Roswell whom Davey had ever hankered after, though plenty had tried to catch his eye.

It rained most of that night, with the rainwater plop-ping down into the pots we'd set under roof leaks. The drops made a little sort of song I listened to while Marilly snored some beside me.

I didn't go back to sleep when the rain ended. I lay there thinking of the days I had pretended to be Hannibal and remembering Rosellen. Suddenly I heard voices outside our shanty. They were men's voices—Davey's and somebody else's. Rolling over, I looked through a crack. The moon was out by now, so I had a good view of the camp. Some of the folk in the camp had gotten so weary of ankle-deep mud in rainy weather that they'd put down old busted-up boards to walk on. One of them led up to our door.

Davey was standing on it. Another man was there, too. It wasn't Gar Redmond this time but somebody taller and thinner and wearing a short, gray soldier jacket.

I could hear Davey telling him, "This is where my folks live. I can't ask you in this late."

"It don't matter, Reed. I got to get back to my own kin." The other man chuckled and added, "Did you take to what you heard tonight at our meetin'?"

"I don't know yet. I'll have to think on it. But I won't never mention it to anybody. Redmond don't need to fear for that. No bluebelly'll ever know."

"Redmond knows you're all right." The man now turned around and left as Davey silently came inside the shack.

A beam of moonlight spread across the floor over to the edge of his mattress. I could see Jem asleep, and I could see something else—Davey's boots. There wasn't one speck of mud on them. Atlanta was plumb full of sticky red mud, so wherever Davey had been tonight, he hadn't been walking. That said only one thing to me—he'd been riding on a horse or in a buggy.

Riding where? Should I tell Mama tomorrow? I could hear her breathing deep and slow, so she was asleep and didn't see Davey come in. Sure as could be, my big brother was up to something. He had secrets from us.

I didn't tell Mama, after all. I didn't want to worry her after Davey told us in the morning he'd escorted Amalie Redmond to a "calico ball." That was the sort of dance where Atlanta ladies served only water for refreshments and wore cotton dresses to prove their loyalty to the South.

I was heavy of heart over Davey, though, and as I walked to work I took more notice of the Yankee soldiers than ever. Sissa walked with me, and we talked about Yankees together. She agreed that the city was as full of bluebellies as fleas on a hound dog's back—standing by themselves, talking to each other or to black men, giving orders to folks, driving wagons, riding their fat, oats-fed horses. Everywhere I looked, I saw bluecoats.

That morning, as always, I gazed over at the hotel, but there wasn't hide nor hair of Delie to be seen. There weren't even any soldiers sitting on the porch, but they'd be out for sure later on, when the day warmed up.

Just as I started up the steps to Mr. Herrick's store, I heard my name called in a voice I didn't know. "You, the Reed girl. Stop a minute."

Up came old Miz Zilphey Sanders with a basket over her arm. It was the first time I'd set eyes on her since our first day in Atlanta. She looked just the same, and wore the same rose-colored dress.

She said to me, "So you Roswell mill folk did stay on here in Atlanta?"

"Yes'm, we did."

She tossed her head. "I'm on my way to the Freedman's Bureau for some food supplies I'm needing. How come I never see you or your mama there?"

I told her proudly, "We don't ever go there. I'm workin', and so is my mama and my brothers. We don't need Yankee help."

This riled her. "The bacon and things they hand out don't poison me, girl. They owe me food for bustin' up my house and killin' my man!" She poked me on the chest with a sharp finger. "Have you seen Amalie lately?"

I nodded. "I seen her awhile back. She come in here where I work to buy cloth."

"Did she have a bluebelly soldier with her?"

I hated to tell Miz Zilphey the truth, but I did. "She come in here with one."

"That big, tall, black-headed one, or the littler one with the straw-colored mustache?"

Remembering the shoulder-straps hunting for Hannibal Sanders, I said, "The one I saw wasn't neither of them."

"Glory be! How many Yankees has she got on her string? Well, she don't come near me no more."

"Why don't she?"

"I tolerated it the first time she fetched me vittles with a Yankee officer ridin' alongside her, but when she come with a diff'rent one the next week, I told her to feed what was in her basket to the bluebellies and never come near me agin. I said I'd ruther go directly to the Freedman's Bureau than take charity from the likes of her. Mark my words, girl, no good will come of her cavortin' about with Yankees."

Remembering how nice Miz Amalie'd been to us Reeds, I tried to stick up for her. "She only does it 'cause she wants 'em to buy from her candy store."

"Nonsense! Don't you believe that for a minute. I been hearin' talk about her and all her soldier friends." Miz Zilphey nodded her head, and as she did, her straw hat teetered down over one eye. After she pushed it up she asked, "How's Marilly? Is she workin' for Yankee money, too?"

"No, ma'am. She stays in our house and takes care of my baby sister."

"Ain't that nice and pleasant for her, though? She don't beg from Yankees." The woman turned away from me.

I called after her. "Do you want me to give your regards to Aunt Marilly?"

That stopped her. She pondered for a minute, then said, "Suit yourself as to that. I take it strange that you call her Aunt Marilla when she ain't no more kin to you than I am."

"We're beholden to Aunt Marilly and fond of her. That's why."

Oh, but I was glad Miz Zilphey didn't live near us.

Strangers at first, Miz Barrows and Sissa were lots better folks than Miz Zilphey would ever be. I'd swear she'd been weaned on pickle brine.

When I told Mama and Aunt Marilly about seeing her that night, they only shook their heads. Seeing her one time had been enough for Mama. Aunt Marilly told us, "She ain't no friend to me or to you Reeds or any Sanderses. She's always been uppity to her kinfolk, and she still is."

Two weeks went by, with all of us working and doing pretty much what we did every day. Davey was learning what he called the Morse Code, Jem was getting ads for the paper, and I was measuring out and cutting cloth, ribbons, and lace. Davey only stayed out real late one night during that time, so Mama grew more easy in her mind about him.

I caught sight of Delie twice, once washing hotel windows and once polishing brass front-door knobs. I spotted Amalie Redmond's bluebelly officers a couple times on the front porch of the hotel, sitting, smoking, and talking, and I figured them to be friends.

I warmed up a bit to Mary Anne and went to her for help with the hardest words in my fairy-tale book. The word *gnome* was truly puzzling. How could that be said *nome* when it had a *g* in front? It gratified me that she didn't know why, either, though she knew how to say the word.

Mostly those two weeks I fretted about money. The year was more than half over, and we didn't have as much as we hoped to have—it cost so dearly to live in Atlanta. We couldn't grow our own vegetables here, and so we had to buy everything.

And then on Monday of the third week my life just plain caved in on me when I was least expecting it. I heard the door bell at the store jingle, and looked up, expecting to see a lady customer. But there he was! My tall, blue-belly shoulder-straps, the cavalry lieutenant from Indiana!

He came right over to me, his blue eyes boring into my brown ones. My heart jumped up into my throat, choking me. I wanted to cut and run, but I couldn't move.

I heard Mr. Herrick ask him, "May I help you, Lieutenant?"

"No, sir, you may not. I have business with this girl here."

"With Hannalee?" Mr. Herrick sounded surprised.

"No, sir, with Hannibal Sanders, the mill-hand bobbin boy this girl pretended to be up in Indiana last year." He talked only to me now. "I know for a fact that you're Hannalee Reed, and I also know for a fact that you used to be the boy, Hannibal Sanders, before you ran away and made your way back to Georgia. Isn't that true, Hannalee—Hannibal? You led me quite a merry chase, but you're not fooling anybody anymore."

I did the only thing I could think to do. I took the

yellow pencil I always kept stuck behind my left ear to do my figuring, and I pushed it at him.

He didn't take it, though. All he did was lean on my counter, his blue elbows on some peach-colored silk, and laugh into my face. I reckoned I was as pale as bleached muslin, I was so scared by now.

It had happened. I was caught! Next he'd haul me off to the Yankee jail house. I was so small and he was so big, he wouldn't have to call for guards with muskets. I couldn't cry out. I was like a bush that had taken root to the spot or a rock in the road wagons ran over. If I tried to talk to him, I knew all I could do was squawk or squeak. I couldn't even think of the words to a prayer.

I poked the pencil at him again.

CHAPTER ELEVEN

Worse Than War

THE SHOULDER-STRAPS ASKED, "WHY DO YOU KEEP shoving that pencil into my face?"

Why? He should know, same as me.

I got out a whisper. "You know danged well why. Please take it and leave me alone." I'd pay Mr. Herrick back for it out of what he paid me.

But the lieutenant wouldn't take the pencil. He just asked again, "Well, are you or aren't you Hannibal Sanders who used to live at Mrs. Burton's house in Cannelton, Indiana?"

He knew the name of the lady I'd boarded with. He must know everything about me. I felt sicker than a dog.

In another whisper I told him, "Yes, sir, I used to call myself Hannibal Sanders. I ran away from Miz Burton's, and I stole a pencil from her, so I know why you came after me. I'm ready to go to jail with you, but let me take off my apron first. It don't belong to me. Here, take the pencil."

He straightened up now. "Pencil? I never heard about any pencil."

I wanted to clap my hands over my mouth. I'd damned myself with my own tongue. Now I'd gone and done it. Well, I'd shut up from now on.

Mr. Herrick was at my side by now. He asked, "What's this all about, Lieutenant? This girl's scared half out of her wits. Who are you and what do you want with her?"

The lieutenant had a wide grin for Mr. Herrick. "Lieutenant Marcus Burton at your service, sir. I hail from Cannelton, Indiana. My mother wrote me when she knew that I'd be stationed here in Atlanta so I could find a mill-hand boy by the name of Hannibal Sanders who used to live with her and who ran away home to Georgia—or that's where she thought he went."

Mr. Herrick asked, "What does your mother want with Hannalee?"

The officer laughed again. "Nothing. She liked the boy. She only wants me to find him and write back to her how he's doing. She figured he went to his family in Roswell. I went there hunting him and learned he didn't exist." He shrugged. "When I wrote her that, she asked a girl mill worker who lives in our house about Hannibal."

I held my breath. Rosellen!

He went on. "That girl confessed to her that Hannibal Sanders wasn't even a boy, but a short-haired girl named Hannalee Reed. I went to Roswell again and learned that the Reeds had come to Atlanta to work. I met Miss Amalie Redmond and came into your store with her just before my mother wrote me her second letter telling me about Hannalee Reed. I remembered this girl, so when I found the time, I came back here."

I thought I'd fall down senseless on the floor. I remembered that Miz Burton had had menfolk serving in the Union Army. This Marcus Burton had to be one of them—even if he didn't take after his mother much in looks.

I asked, "Didn't she tell you I stole a pencil when I left?"

"No, she said you were hot for learning things, and she liked that in you. She asked me to find out if you needed anything, and if you did, I was to help you out."

Help me out? I couldn't believe my ears. I said, "Us Reeds are doin' fine here. Thank your ma for me, and tell her I'm grateful to her. She was a real nice lady. I didn't know there was Yankees like her."

Then I felt heat rise up in my face at what awfulness had popped out of me.

Lieutenant Burton only laughed, and so did Mr. Herrick and Mary Anne. To cover up my bad words I asked him, "Did your ma say anything about the girl that told her who I really was?"

He said, "No, she didn't. And since I haven't been home in two years' time, I never set eyes on her myself." He slapped the counter softly with his big brown hand, then said, "Well, that's that. The lost is found, and I'll go about my business. In my next letter I'll tell my mother that you are well. Good luck to you, Miss Hannalee Reed."

Miz Burton's son tipped his black slouch hat to me and to Mary Anne like we was grown-up ladies, and out he went, his cavalry saber swinging at his side.

Once he was gone, I plumb melted down and busted into tears. Rather than have them drop onto the silk, I ran for the back porch and bawled out of happiness.

After I'd been out there a spell the back door opened, and out came Mary Anne. Without a word she sat down, put her arm around me, and pulled my head over onto her warm shoulder. She smelled of cinnamon. I soon found out why. She took a soft, cinnamon-flavored cookie out of her pinafore pocket and handed it to me. It tasted half salty from my tears and half spicy from the cinnamon.

Oh, the Herricks had surely been kind to me when I'd been so scared. Mr. Herrick, I could tell, had been ready to put up an argument on my behalf.

Mary Anne told me, "Papa says to tell you that you don't have to come back to work now if you don't feel like it. Sit out here and admire Marengo, our horse. Papa says you just had a really bad time, and we understand."

"Thank you kindly, Mary Anne," I said. "I'd like to wait out here with your horse and you till my eyes ain't red. Then I'll be back inside."

"Hannalee, can I ask you something? How could any-one have thought you were a boy with your long hair?"

"This hair ain't mine. I had to cut it off. What's in this snood is mostly Mama's hair."

Mary Anne gasped. "It isn't all yours? Why, not a soul would ever know that!"

"Thank you kindly for sayin' that." Pleased with what she'd said, I patted Mama's hair and changed the subject. "Why did you name your horse Marengo? I rode a horse one time. Jem and me called him Thunder."

"Papa named him after Napoleon's horse. Lots of horses are named that."

After resting for a time I went back to work and mea-sured cloth the rest of the day, feeling as calm as could be after my fearful scare.

I mostly ran home that night, going as fast as my feet would take me. Sissa Barrows spotted me going by, but with her limp she couldn't catch up to me.

I called back to her, "Sissa, I'll tell you later why I'm in such a great big hurry."

Mama wasn't home yet, but Aunt Marilly and Jem were. I plunked both of them down on stools Davey had made for us from wood scraps, and told them all about Lieutenant Burton.

Jem laughed out loud, and Marilly shook her head and said, "Well, I'm surely glad that's over, Hannalee. I never knowed you called yourself Sanders there."

"That wasn't my idea. It was Rosellen's. And she called herself Rosellen Reed, not Sanders."

"Well, that does beat all. She took on Davey's name!" said the old lady. "Does your mama know that?"

"No, I didn't want to tell her. It'd only make her heart sad."

Marilly warned, "You'd best not tell Davey. It'd cut him to the quick. It proves that she loved him then."

"We won't ever let him know—not any one of us," I told her.

When Mama came in, I told my story all over again, and I watched her first frown, then smile at me. She said softly, "You never told me you stole a pencil, Hannalee."

"Mama, it was truly only half of a pencil."

"No matter, it was stealin'. What did the Yankee officer have to tell you about Rosellen?"

"Only what I told you jest now."

She nodded. "I'm glad as could be that this worry's off our minds, but if you see him agin, ask if he's gotten another letter from the North, and if there's anythin' in it about Rosellen."

"Oh, Mama, I'd be scared to do that."

"Why? Didn't he say he wanted to help us out?"

"What should I ask him?"

"If the mill girl is called Rosellen, and how she's farin'." Mama looked to Aunt Marilly. "Marilly, if she's still livin' as a boarder in that Yankee house, it don't appear to me that she's got married to anybody up north."

I said, "All right. I'll ask him. What if Rosellen's still not wedded? Should we tell Davey that?"

Marilly said, "Best not to. She's been writ to that he's dead. That's how he says he wants it."

I sighed. What she had said was the truth. I'd penned a letter to her with that very stolen pencil. Maybe she'd gotten it, maybe not—but all the same, she'd never come home again. Davey told me he wouldn't take at all to writing her that he was alive and one-armed.

I said, "Rosellen cared enuf about me to tell Miz Burton what to tell her son so he could find me and help me out. I say that proves she ain't forgot us."

"Rosellen won't never forget any of us" came sadly from Marilly.

Naturally, because I was looking for him now, I didn't see Lieutenant Burton anywhere during the next two weeks, though I did catch sight of the two officers who seemed to court Miz Amalie. They often stood together on the hotel steps, pulling on their gloves before they mounted their horses.

By now I'd finished reading my fairy-tale book and would soon be starting in on a new and harder one Mary Anne had promised to lend me. I'd taken it into my head to lend my first book to Delie—if she felt up to trying it. Even if she couldn't read it yet, she could look at the pictures of princesses and dragons and wizards and elves. Since I hadn't caught sight of her during this time, I planned to go to the Beaufort Hotel after I had my cornbread lunch, rap on the rear door, and ask for her by name. All they could do was shoo me away if they didn't want me nearby. I figured I'd go at noon, not only because that was my free time but because I thought it'd be when Delie had lunch, too.

When I told Mary Anne what I was going to do, she said, "That's a dandy thing to do, Hannalee. I've noticed that black girl, too. She's very pretty. I tried to talk to her once when she was on the hotel porch, but all she did was look at me and go inside with the broom she was sweeping with."

I nodded. "She's shy. I don't think Delie would have talked to me neither, except that I did her a favor." And now I told about the boys' throwing mud on the hotel laundry.

It was Mary Anne's turn to nod. She said, "I've seen those bad boys. What they need is a school to go to. Is Delie learning to read, too?"

"She says she is. She's sort of teachin' herself—gettin' on to words the way Davey is by studyin' telegraphin'. She sure wants to read."

"It's very hard to teach yourself. Papa says there'll be schools here real soon—schools for black children, he means."

"Not for you and me?" I was disappointed.

"Not for a while. It's more important that the black people go so they can catch up—they've been kept down so very long. Papa says it was a shame that the only schools Atlanta ever had were for white boys and girls and were the kind where parents had to pay to let their children in. He believes in free schooling for everybody."

I heaved a sigh. "So do I. Jest as soon as ever I can, I want to go to a real school. I never been to one."

She touched my arm. "But all the same, you're doing just fine."

"I want to be a teacher someday."

"So do I. You'll probably be a better one than I am, because your schooling came so hard to you."

"Oh, I dunno. Mebbe not." All the same, her words had pleasured me.

A little after twelve o'clock I crossed the street, snaking my way among carts and riders. I went alongside the Beaufort Hotel to the back and knocked on the door. A tall black man in a white jacket answered it.

"Yes?" was all he said.

"I'd like to see Delie Brackett. Can she come outside?"

"I'll see if she wants to." Then he closed the door in my face.

After a few minutes Delie came out. She was chewing on a chicken leg. She said, "Oh, Hannalee."

"Uh-huh. I jest got done with readin' this here fairy-tale book. Mebbe you'd like to have a borrow of it?"

She sat down on the top step, and so did I. As she ate, she looked through the first twenty or so pages of the book.

"It's mighty fine," she told me after a while. "I can't make out most of the words, but I like the pictures."

"It's about princesses and fairies and castles and things like that."

She nodded. "I like to hear about princesses and scary things like giants, but I like happy endings most of all."

"So do I." I got up to go. "Do them boys pester you anymore?"

"No. The man who owns the hotel told their pas to keep 'em home, or he'd take a whip to their hides."

I said, "Good. I like my job now. Do you like yours? I seen you clean spittoons."

Delie got up with my book under her arm. "No, that's hateful work. I don't much like what I got to do here. We need the money, though. Ma don't get as much as we need from the Freedman's Bureau, and it costs a lot to live in Atlanta. Workin' in this hotel is rough. The menfolk I have to work around is rough—hard drinkers and cussers, too. The saloon's open all night long, and it can be mighty loud down there."

I asked, "Yankee officers, you mean?"

"Not jest them—other menfolk—some of 'em from

the North, others from these parts. I seen that one-armed brother of yours there, too, with some other men. I don't go home to Ma and my sister nights 'cause it's too dangerous to go to the camp by my lonesome." She pointed to the top floor of the hotel. "I got me a little room up there to sleep in. The noise from down below gets so loud sometimes, I can't hardly rest at all. I only go home on Sunday mornin's in the daylight."

So this was where Davey was some nights. I'd tell Mama what I'd learned. I said to Delie, "I'm allus home before dark, too. Keep the book long as you need to. I'm startin' in on another one."

My book held to her chest, she asked me, "How come you're bein' so kindly to me?"

I considered a bit before I answered, hunting for the right true words. "I had real hard times last year, and things ain't easy for me now, but there's been folks, pure strangers, that have been good to me when I didn't expect any goodness from anybody. I reckon you could say I was passin' their goodness to me onto you 'cause I seen you in trouble with them mud-throwin' boys."

She didn't say a word. She just stood there with my book while I ran around the corner of the hotel heading for Mr. Herrick's store. I didn't want to get her into trouble for being out too long on the back steps.

Three more days went by without my spotting my Yankee shoulder-straps. I asked Miz Barrows if he still came to visit the Yankee ladies she sewed for, and she said he hadn't been there for a while. The girl he'd seemed sort of smitten with had gotten herself engaged to another officer, so naturally that would be why he stopped visiting.

Saturday night we celebrated that my troubles with the Yankee lieutenant were over by having a hen for supper. It was an old one Aunt Marilly cooked with corn and turnip greens and dried peas, and it was mighty tasty. Even with the Barrowses sharing our meal, Mama saved a leg for Davey in case he came home hungry later on. But Davey didn't come home that night at all!

Because I was weary, I fell asleep fast, but I came bolt awake when I heard the hard pounding on the door to our shack. My heart nearly busted out of my chest. I'd heard that sound before. It wasn't no human hand knocking on our door. No, it was the butt end of a pistol! That was how the bluebellies had knocked on our door in Roswell before they came in and dragged Jem and me away to the North.

Mama cried out, "I'm comin'! I'm comin'!" Then, "Hannalee, you light a candle."

I had matches and a candle beside my bed, so I did what she asked. Then I followed her to the door with Jem behind me. The night was dark—so dark, I couldn't see the face of the big man in the doorway, but the candle glow showed me the U.S. on his belt and the gold bars on his shoulder straps. A Yankee soldier! Other shadowy men were crowded behind him.

He asked Mama, "Is there a man by the name of Garson Redmond here?"

Mama told him calmly, "Mr. Redmond don't live here. You got the wrong place."

"Are you named Reed?"

"That's right."

"Well, your son David Reed's in our custody right now. We're looking for Redmond, too."

"In custody?" cried Mama. At that moment her face looked just the way it had our last day in Roswell when I asked her if her Indian blood saw bad things ahead for us. Her blood had told her truly.

The Yankee said, "Yes, we're holding him for murder."

I yelled, "*Murder?* Davey wouldn't kill nobody."

"It appears he may have—a federal army officer, at that. He and Redmond may have been in on it together. A major of the Union Army was shot to death at the Beaufort Hotel tonight. A witness says he saw David Reed fire the pistol."

Mama cried, "He hasn't got a pistol!"

"Redmond had. We have reason to believe he loaded it for your son, and your son fired it. Now, is Redmond here? He left the hotel before your son was taken away."

"Nobody's here but us womenfolk and my boy," Mama told the officer in a dull voice. "Come in and look around. You'd be doin' that, anyway, wouldn't you?"

"Yes, ma'am, we have to."

I started to tremble. Davey had killed a Yankee. This was worse than Jem and me being sent north. This was lots worse than the war had been for us. They could hang Davey fast, and they had a whole army here in Georgia to do it.

CHAPTER TWELVE

Help?

THE SEVEN YANKEES LOOKED THROUGH OUR SHACK, even lifting up our mattresses. Of course, they didn't find anything. As they were leaving, Mama asked, "Where's my boy bein' held?"

"In the jail up by the courthouse."

"Can I see him?"

"That depends on the provost marshal. You can go and ask him. Do you have any idea where Redmond is? You'd better tell us if you do."

"No, we haven't got any notion. We almost never set eyes on him. He don't come to our camp. He don't like it here."

A Yankee laughed. "It isn't hard to see why such a fine Rebel gent wouldn't. It stinks hereabouts."

Jem flared. "We don't like how it smells no better'n you do."

"Hush, Jem," ordered Mama.

Once the soldiers had gone, she herded Jem and me to her. Marilly stood very close by holding Paulina, who'd woke up and was yelling.

I asked, "Oh, Mama, what'll we do? I jest know they figure to hang Davey."

Mama let out a sigh that began at the soles of her feet. "We got to swallow our pride and ask for help—Yankee help. Tomorrow mornin' I'll tell Mr. Levy what the bluebellies said about Davey, and ask him what we ought to do."

I said, "I could ask Mr. Herrick or Lieutenant Burton."

Jem nodded. "I'll ask the men I know at the newspaper."

"No, children. Let me start with Mr. Levy. He told me he studied the law a long time back."

I burst in with, "Mama, let's go see Amalie Redmond first of all. She's got plenty of Yankee friends."

Aunt Marilly's words were bitter. "If they're lookin' for her brother, she won't be havin' Yankee friends no more. And there's somethin' else—Delia, you and the young'uns might not have jobs with Yankees no more, either."

Mama agreed. "That's the Lord's truth, Marilly, although we must hope for the best. Let's sit down and keep real close together till it's time for me to fix us some breakfast and go to Mr. Levy."

I asked, "If Davey's supposed to have shot a bluebelly officer, how come they're huntin' for Gar Redmond, too?"

"Didn't you hear that Yankee who was jest here? They think Redmond's got a part in the shootin', too. Davey couldn't load a pistol with jest one hand, could he? But Redmond could have done that and gave it to him."

I said, "Davey's too smart to do that. I don't think he killed anybody."

Jem came in with, "I can find out a lot about what happened tonight." He twisted away from where we were huddled together, all hunkered down on Mama's mattress. "The newspaper office stays open all night long. They'll know what went on."

Now Jem tucked his nightshirt into his trousers, put on his shoes without even lacing them up, and ran out the door while Mama and the rest of us sat silent.

She said, "Let him go. He can take care of hisself, and mebbe he'll bring us some comfortin' news."

Jem came home close to day-peep. One look at his face by candlelight told me he wasn't fetching comfort. It was long and sour. He was panting, he'd run so fast.

He told us, gasping, "It happened at the Beaufort Hotel like them Yankees said it did. They was all in the drinkin' saloon—two Yankee shoulder-straps, Davey and Gar, and some other men. Davey and Redmond got to arguin' with one of the Yankee officers about a paper on the wall askin' that folks give money to help out President Jeff Davis's fam'ly. They're poor and suff'rin' and deservin'. Gar nailed the paper up. A Yankee officer tore it down, and Redmond called him a cuss-word name. Davey got Gar to put the paper back up, and the Yankees left it there. Then Redmond told the two Yankees he didn't want neither of 'em courtin' his sister. Then he hit one of the Yankees that'd started cussin' him out."

I asked, "What did Davey do?"

"Nothin' yet. Gar threw his whiskey glass into one Yankee's face and ran out of the bar. The other men who were there had all left at the start of the trouble. That left jest Davey there with the two bluebellies. One of the Yankees—the captain it was—hit Davey and dragged him by his good arm out into a hallway beside the saloon. The men at the newspaper figger he meant to beat Davey up good, 'cause Redmond had gone and he couldn't get at him. The other Yankee shoulder-straps went with him. The hallway's a real dark place."

I told Mama, "It is. I went down it one time. It's narrow and dark as sin."

"Well, there was the sound of a pistol and the noise of somebody fallin' down, then the sound of somebody else fallin'. The Yankee captain came runnin' back into the saloon yellin' that the one-armed Reb had shot his friend, Major Fenton. That brought hotel folks runnin' into the saloon, and one of 'em went for more Yankee soldiers."

Major Fenton? My memory went back to the day we all visited Miz Amalie's store. That'd been the name of the officer who'd needed the horehound lozenges.

Jem went on. "The Yankee who got shot was the

yellow-mustached one I saw Miz Amalie ridin' with outside town. The captain's named Hartford."

For sure, that was the bluebelly from the candy store, and both of them lived at the Beaufort Hotel.

Jem was still talking. "Captain Hartford said after he saw Davey take the pistol from his pocket and fire it, he kicked it out of Davey's hand and hit Davey hard as he could and knocked him out. It was a Confederate Army pistol. He's also sayin' Davey killed the major 'cause he was jealous of him and wanted Amalie for hisself."

"Oh, Davey!" Mama said mournfully.

We waited in deep pain that long, long, hot Sunday for Mama to come home. Because she'd been away till suppertime, we all got hopeful and reckoned she'd had some luck with Mr. Levy.

The minute we saw her, we knew otherwise, though. She'd been weeping. As I helped her unlace her shoes to ease her swelled-up feet, I asked, "Did you see Davey?"

"I surely did, but they only gave me five minutes. Mr. Levy done all he could to get me inside the jail by writin' a letter for me. He's a real fine man and not scared of soldiers and their laws. He says he wants me to stay on workin' for him, no matter what."

"What about Davey, Mama?"

"He's got a big bump on his jaw. He says he don't recall nothin' that took place after the Yankee officer hustled him out into the hallway. They was all pretty well lik-kered up."

"That figgers," snapped Marilly.

"Davey says he don't really recall shootin' anybody. He never had no pistol, though Gar did. Davey seen it. He don't recall if Gar left with it or slipped it into Davey's coat pocket. That's what the Yankees think happened. They'll be holdin' Davey for a trial, though they're still huntin' Redmond and some other men. They think they're Reg-ulators. If they catch 'em, they'll hang 'em."

"Like they'll hang Davey," said Jem bitterly.

Angry by now, I asked, "Oh, what'll we do?"

Mama said, "There ain't nothin' we *can* do. Jest sit and wait for the trial. Mr. Levy says it'll be a all-soldier trial, 'cause it was a Yankee officer that got killed. He said the big witness aginst Davey is the bluebelly officer, Captain Hartford."

I'd never felt so low before—not even on the mill work-ers' prison train going to the North.

I said, "I don't s'pose it'd do any good to talk to Mr. Herrick about helpin' Davey, would it?"

"No, Hannalee. I jest pray he won't take away your job. And leave that Indiana shoulder-straps alone, too. He won't be so friendly to you now."

"No, I reckon not. When's the trial to be?"

"Pretty soon—in a week."

"Can the rest of us go see Davey?"

"No, the Yankees won't let children in. I already asked. I'm his ma, so I can go see him when they'll let me. It'd be diff'rent if he had a wife. She could go see him, too."

Bitterness rose up in me as I said, "It'd all be diff'rent for us if Davey'd married Rosellen last year when she wanted him to."

"Amen to that," came from Marilly. "She'd have kept him out of drinkin' saloons where there's nothin' much but misery to be found."

Bad as we all felt, Mama, Jem, and I went to work same as ever Monday morning. I felt in my bones that everybody in Atlanta was reading in the newspaper about Davey and Redmond. With every step I took, I felt folks eyeing me.

The Herricks were friendly to me. They didn't say one word about Davey all morning long, and I was grateful to them.

At noontime I went out as usual onto the back steps to eat and was pleased that Mary Anne let me be. As I sat down I noticed something, though—my book of fairy tales was on the top step. Delie had put it there. Was this her way of saying she didn't want any part of me because my big brother had shot a Yankee, part of the army that had freed her?

Suddenly I took note that the book was open to the first story—the one about a brother and sister and a wicked

witch who wanted to kill and eat them. How come Delie
hadn't brought back my book closed?

I looked at the first page, and what I saw made me get
mad—words were underlined in black ink. By all the
Holy Hokies, markings in ink on my only book!

I read the words, boiling with anger. Wait! Wait a second, though! She'd underlined the word *brother,* then the
word *not,* and finally the word *kill.* Easy words she probably could read—easy as pie for me. I read aloud, "Brother
not kill."

Brother not kill!

All at once I knew what she'd done. Delie lived at the
hotel. She knew Davey was my brother. This was a
message—a message for me about him.

I let out a yell, jumped up, and ran inside. I grabbed
hold of Mary Anne and dragged her out. She read the
three words, then listened to what I had to tell her.

Then she said slowly, "She's telling you that she knows
your brother is innocent. The only way she'd know that is
if she saw what happened. How would she know that
otherwise?"

"That's right, Mary Anne. She seen somethin'! She
knows somethin'!"

"Hannalee, let's go over to the hotel to see her. Do you
know where to find her?"

"Sure I do. We go 'round to the back door and ask for
her. She'll come right out, like when I gave her a loan of

my book. She must want to see me, or she wouldn't have fetched my book back to me marked up the way it is. She's real shy, so she wouldn't have fetched it to your front door."

Putting the book under my arm, I crossed the street with Mary Anne to the hotel. We skirted the side of the building and went to the back, where I rapped on the door just like before.

The same black porter answered it, and asked me, "What do you want now, gal?"

"To see Delie—same as I wanted last time."

"Delie ain't here no more. She must have left in the middle of last night. She took what she owned out of her room in a gunnysack, and she ran off. The night baker saw her skedaddle."

Mary Anne asked, "Did she say anything to the baker?"

"He said all she had to say was that she wasn't goin' to live anyplace anymore where real bad things happened downstairs like jest happened Saturday night."

I wanted to know, "Where did she go to?"

He shifted his feet like he was weary of me and Mary Anne. "Don't ask me, gals. The night baker said she didn't tell him. Delie jest up and left."

"Where would she go?" asked Mary Anne, turning to me.

"Where her folks live—in the camp out on Decatur Road."

The hotel man shook his head. "That'd be a bad place to go. There's smallpox out there."

Smallpox? I remembered hearing of it being in the blacks' camp when we first came to Atlanta. Nothing scared me so much as that evil sickness. No, that wasn't right. Something else scared me more—the terrible trouble Davey was in. His hanging scared me more!

Mary Anne asked me, "What'll you do now, Hannalee?"

I knew what, although just thinking about it gave me the shivers. After I thanked the porter and he'd shut the door, I told my friend, "I got to go to the Decatur Road camp and look for Delie. Tell your papa for me what's goin' on, and why I got to go away this afternoon."

"But that camp's quite a distance south of here, isn't it?"

"Yes. It'll be a long walk there and back, but I got to do it. My big brother's life is at stake."

"Can't you get your mother or somebody to go with you?"

"I could, Mary Anne, but it'd take time for me to get to Mr. Levy's house, get her, and then walk out to Decatur Road. If Delie saw somethin' the other night at the hotel, she might not stay at the camp. Mebbe she saw the shootin' and knows who did it. Mebbe she's scared of that person 'cause she's a . . ." I didn't know the right word.

Mary Anne did. "Witness, you mean." Suddenly she snapped her fingers. "I know what we'll do. We'll both go to Decatur Road. We'll ride Marengo there. Come on."

Grabbing me by the hand, she and I raced across the street, making a horse rear and nearly throw its rider.

Behind the shop, Mary Anne bridled and saddled the horse. Then she ran inside and came back wearing a sunbonnet. She said, "I took a dollar from my tin bank. Nobody should ever go anywhere without money. And I left a note for Papa saying that I was going away for a time with you to take your mind off your troubles."

"Did you tell your pa where we're headed and why?"

"No. I let him think we're just going for a horseback ride. Hannalee, do you think I'd dare tell him where we're going? He'd tell me I couldn't go. He'd go find soldiers and tell them about Delie's message. Then they'd go to the hotel, talk to people there, and hours and hours later they'd start to look for Delie. I know how long it takes grownups to do things sometimes. They're so careful, they lose lots of time."

Amazed at her bravery, I asked, "But what about the smallpox?"

"Oh, I've been inoculated against it. We won't go inside any houses there. I don't think you can catch diseases in the open air. Come on, Hannalee. Help me mount up, then you take my hand and I'll pull you up behind me."

"Oh, Mary Anne!"

My heart was so full of gratitude, I couldn't say another word, not even "Thank you."

She talked, though, as we trotted out onto the street.

"This is a real adventure, isn't it? I haven't had an adventure in a long time."

As we jolted along south out of Atlanta, I told her all about Davey and Rosellen. When I'd finished, she sighed. "That's the saddest, most romantic story I ever listened to, and it's true, too. Is Rosellen pretty?"

"When she smiles, she's like an angel, Mary Anne."

"An angel? Just think of that. And she's lost to him forever."

CHAPTER THIRTEEN

Decatur Road and Beyond

I DIDN'T EXPECT THE CAMP FOR THE BLACK PEOPLE TO BE any nicer than our camp was, but I couldn't believe how much worse it was. There were shanties here, too, but they appeared more to be old boards tied together than nailed the way our place was. Some of them didn't have tin roofs at all, but old knotty boards put on every which way. There were smoking campfires and clotheslines, but what flapped on them was more raggedy than what we had on ours. Like our camp, it smelled bad, too—the same smell of unburied, rotting stuff and privies that needed quicklime put in them.

"Oh, my gosh!" Mary Anne said. "This place smells terribly bad, Hannalee."

In spite of her kindness I couldn't help but tell her, "You never came to where I live, so you wouldn't know how bad it smells there—jest like this."

There weren't many black men in sight. Mostly I saw women and children, and they all seemed to have come to stand in their doorways and stare at us.

"What you want?" cried out a thin, old, gray-headed

man in a ragged pair of overalls. "We don't need no little white gals here."

A tall woman came out of the same shack to stand behind him. She told us, "You'll fetch us trouble here, and mebbe some for yourself, too. Git back where you belong. They's smallpox here in this place. It's mighty catchin'."

Mary Anne shouted, "We won't be here long. We're hunting for a girl our age named Delie. She lives here. She used to work at the Beaufort Hotel."

The man shook his head. "I don't know anybody by that name, and if'n I did, I wouldn't tell the pair of you."

Mary Anne wasn't fazed. She told him, "It's very important that we find Delie. We don't mean her any harm. We don't want to have to send any soldiers here. They'll be hunting up missing hotel workers soon."

"Lincoln soldiers? Riled up 'cause of Delie?" The tall woman looked at the old man. She touched his arm and said, "We don't want no soldiers here, not even Lincoln army ones." She came up to Marengo. "Don't be scared of us. I ain't got the smallpox." She pointed. "See that shack over there, the one with the green board in the middle of the back? There used to be a young gal name of Delie livin' there with her folks. I ain't seen her for a long time now, but her mama is still there."

"Thank you. Thank you very much," came from Mary Anne as she loosened the reins and nudged Marengo forward to the shack in the distance.

Once we were there, we slid down off Marengo. I
stood by him while Mary Anne went up to the door and
knocked on it. Was she ever a bold piece! I wondered if all
Yankee girls from Connecticut were like her.

A pretty-faced black girl who looked like Delie came to
the door and stuck her head out. I saw the fear flash in her
eyes as she looked first at Mary Anne, then at me. Then
her dark eyes narrowed.

"Who are you? What do you want?" she asked us
sharply.

Mary Anne swung around and pointed at me. "We
want Delie. This is her friend, Hannalee Reed. Hannalee
works for my papa across the street from the Beaufort
Hotel. Delie left her a message before she ran away."

The black girl, who had a red bandanna tied around her
neck, came outside now. "What makes you think anybody named Delie lives here?"

I spoke up now for the first time. "The folks over there
said she did." I pointed now. "Delie told me her fam'ly
lived out here in this camp. I reckoned this is where she
came when she left the hotel."

"You're from these parts, ain't you?" asked the black
girl. "I can tell the yellow-headed one's a Yankee, but you
sure ain't. How come Delie'd make friends with the likes
of you?"

" 'Cause I gave her the loan of a book and 'cause I
helped her out once. Her and me was gettin' to be friends

before she got scared by somethin' she saw at the hotel and run away. Ain't you Delie's big sister? You sure look a lot like her."

The girl was quiet for a minute, then she said, "Uh-huh, I'm her sister. She ain't here, though."

I asked, "Where did she go, then?"

"I don't aim to tell you, white gal. That's Delie's business. Go away. This camp's for black folks."

I felt tears coming into my eyes. I said, "Oh, please! My brother's in the most terrible trouble in Atlanta. Men say he killed somebody. I know he didn't, though. *Delie knows!* Delie as good as told me he didn't do it. I got to talk with her."

Mary Anne told the sister, "Please help Hannalee. If you try to close your door, I'll put my foot in it while she rides back to get soldiers. They'll come here to ask why Delie ran off from the hotel."

The girl was mad clean through now. "Put your foot in the door, Yankee gal, and I'll stomp on it! Why should I help somebody from the South like your friend here? Folks like her made slaves out of me and my family."

I cried out, "I never did! I was a mill hand from Roswell. We didn't ever have slaves."

Delie's sister asked Mary Anne in a hard voice, "Is what this girl says gospel true?"

"Yes, it is. If Delie isn't here, is your mama home?"

"Uh-huh."

"Can we talk to her?"

"If she'll come out. I'll see." The door was shut hard, and we waited and waited.

Finally it opened, and a big woman in a blue-flowered calico wrapper and carpet slippers came out with the girl beside her. Her voice was deep and soft. "Lucy tells me you come here lookin' for my Delie?"

I told her, "That's right. Can I tell you, please, why I need her so bad?"

"Go ahead, gal. I'm listenin' to you. We'll go set down over there by the fire and talk. There ain't never no cause to stand up when a body can sit down. I reckon this is goin' to take some time of talkin'."

So that's where the four of us went. We sat down beside the big iron pot that held their boiling wash. It smelled of homemade lye soap, the same kind Mama used. It was not a nice odor but a familiar one, and it comforted me some. Delie's ma took the one sawed-off stump there as her seat while the rest of us sat down on the hot red dirt.

"Talk," ordered the older woman.

I did do just that. I told Delie's kinfolk all about how I got to know her, and about the trouble us Reeds were in. My last words were, "I got to find out what made Delie leave the hotel. Ain't she here with you?"

"No, she ain't, child." Delie's ma shook her head. I could see her daughters got their good looks from her. "She surely did upset Lucy and me. Delie come home in the middle of the night actin' scareder than I ever seen her before. She jest sat and shivered. She wouldn't tell us one word what it was about. She was so scared, she could hardly talk at all. Before day-peep she fixed herself a bundle, took some food, and lit out of here while Lucy and me was asleep, worn out with worryin' over her. The night before, she said bluecoat soldiers might be comin' here after her and for us not to say nothin' at all to 'em. We don't want no trouble with the Lincoln soldiers. The Freedman's Bureau feeds us 'cause Delie don't make enough for the three of us. I been sick, so I can't look for work right now, and Lucy can't find enuf sewin' to keep us fed."

From the little bit Delie had told her ma, I figured she must have seen something. I knew it! I asked, "Where would she go?"

Miz Brackett and Lucy looked at each other. Then Delie's mama said, "There ain't but one place she'd go to—if she ever made it to there. I'm worried sick she won't."

Lucy laughed sour as crab apples and spoke to me. "Delie could have got caught by some of you white Georgia folks and put on a boat and sold as a slave in Cuba. We heard tell it's bein' done to black folks who're free now."

I gasped. I hadn't heard that. It made Mary Anne mad. She stormed, "Wait till I tell my papa that!"

I said, "I wouldn't make a slave out of anybody. My

pap didn't hold with slavery one bit. Oh, please, where did Delie go?"

Her ma bent her head and looked at her hands. She sighed, lifted her head, and said, "In this state blacks can't speak out aginst a white man in front of a judge. It's aginst the state law. So Delie can't talk aginst the real killer."

Mary Anne exploded. "Not anymore, it isn't. You're talking about going to a court of law. Papa said just the other day that what a black man or woman says in court holds just as good now as what a white one does. He and I talk about things like that."

"Delie don't know that, Yankee gal."

I said, "I didn't, neither." Then I asked again, "Oh, please, where did she go?"

Her ma looked at me hard and sad. "I can see you don't mean her harm. I know where she'd go—the only other place she knows besides Atlanta. She's gone back to the plantation where I used to be the cook and Lucy and Delie housemaids."

"Where's that?" asked Mary Anne.

"Ma! Don't tell 'em," cried Lucy.

"No, Lucy, it's fittin' that I should tell 'em." The woman gazed at me again. "White gal, what if Delie has to tell you that your brother killed the Yankee officer? What if that's the truth? Mebbe she only give you a message in a book to make you feel better in your mind. Delie's

God-fearin' and truthful mostly, but she's got a kind heart, too. She won't tell you lies you want to hear if you catch up with her."

First I bit my lower lip. Then, remembering the message, I said, "No, I think Delie told me true in the book. In my heart I know Davey didn't kill anybody. I'm bein' hopeful of that."

Delie's ma nodded. "Trust what your heart tells you and keep hopeful." She turned to her daughter beside her. "Lucy, you were raised up God-fearin', too. Don't you say nothin' more aginst what I decide to do. My heart says to me that what this Yankee gal tells us about the judges and the law changin' is true. So I'll tell you how to find your way to Bracketts' plantation. It ain't but twelve miles south by east of here. We had white folks there that liked us. If Delie ain't gone there, I can't tell you where she did go."

After Miz Brackett told us where to go, Mary Anne got up and said, "Come on, Hannalee. We've got the directions. We'll go to that plantation right now. We can be there and back on Marengo before sunset if we don't act lazy about it."

As she went out to the horse I stayed behind a minute with Delie's mama and sister. I told them, "Thank you for what you're doin' for me and my kinfolk. I wish I could pay you back, but I don't see how. I ain't got any money."

The woman folded her hands over her stomach. "Delie told us how you helped her one time. It appears to me she could owe you somethin'." She nodded. "I hope you find her. Tell the Yankee gal to keep to the edges in this here camp. Go 'round it—not through it. The smallpox is mostly in the middle, in the places marked with red paint on the doors."

"Thank you. Thank you agin. God bless you all." I whirled and ran to where Mary Anne was already in the saddle, holding out her hand to pull me up on Marengo.

There were as many wagons coming into Atlanta from the south as us Reeds had seen coming into it from the north last June. Folks who passed us looked at Mary Anne and me with curiosity, but we were left alone until we got to a crossroad where Delie's ma had said we were to turn to the east.

That's where the bluebelly cavalry came cantering up to us. The officer in charge called a halt and rode up to Marengo to ask, "What're you two girls doing with a horse as fine as that?"

Mary Anne knew how to talk back to him. She said, "If you think we stole him, we didn't. He belongs to me and my papa. We live in Atlanta and are in business there. We're from Connecticut."

Because he caught the Yankee accent, the officer laughed. "Don't say another word. I know you're from Connecticut, all right. I hail from New York. Have you seen a rider, a big man with reddish hair, anywhere you've been?"

I sucked in my breath. Gar Redmond, for a fact. The Yankees were out looking for him. I said, being careful, "That sure sounds like Miz Amalie Redmond's brother."

"It is, little girl." The officer rode closer. "You aren't from Connecticut, are you?"

"No," agreed Mary Anne. "This is Hannalee, my Georgia friend."

The officer, a long-faced man with a dark beard, asked me, "What do you know about Redmond?"

I answered, "Miz Amalie gave me some candy one time and I saw him in their store. He was nice to me. Why's the cavalry lookin' for him?"

"For our own special reasons, my girl."

Just as I'd reckoned, they wouldn't tell me, but then I already knew. I was glad to watch the troopers leave, riding west while Mary Anne and I took Marengo east.

We could tell real easy that old General Sherman and his army had been through this part of the country. Over and over in the distance I could see tall, soot-blackened chimneys standing alone, marking where houses had been. Lots of trees had been chopped down, big old ones judging by the size of their stumps. Many fences had been busted apart, and fields that had been planted with corn and cotton now had weeds and brambles and tiny little seedling trees starting up in them.

Our easterly road turned off onto the little country lane Miz Brackett had told us of. It wasn't wide, and both sides were high with wild roses and brambles. Lucky for us, some bramble bushes had ripe berries on them. Hungry by now, we got off the horse and picked some. We ate them and fed a big handful to Marengo.

The Brackett plantation was at the very end of the road. The house was still standing. It was white with a dark green roof and a wide front veranda. At first I thought that the Yankees hadn't come here, but on my second look I could tell that they had. There were some raw-wood tree stumps in front of the house that had probably once been big oaks, and I could see by the black marks on their fronts that two of the smaller houses behind the big one had been set fire to. What had been a nice, high, white-wood fence on one side of the house was smashed in a couple of places so that it had gaps in it.

A lanky boy with soft brown hair came down off the veranda to meet Mary Anne and me. He was dressed in a ruffle-front white shirt and blue pants with a stripe down the side. He came straight up to Marengo and gawked at us with bright hazel-green eyes, like Mary Anne and I had come down off the moon only a few minutes before.

I reckoned we did look a mite strange—Mary Anne in her lilac taffeta dress, white sunbonnet, and white tassel boots, and me in my old blue calico and heavy black shoes, both of us on a good horse that trotted as fine as a razor.

The boy did a strange thing. He bowed, put his hand over his chest like it was a hat, and said, "I'm Henry

Brackett. Who would you ladies be and what brings you here?"

"Lady"? Me, Hannalee Reed, the Roswell bobbin girl, was being called that?

Mary Anne spoke up first. She sounded surprised at the fancy way he talked. "I'm Mary Anne Herrick. I used to live in Connecticut, and now I live in Atlanta. This is my friend, Hannalee Reed, from Atlanta, too."

He asked, "What brings you way out here from Atlanta?"

I'd taken note that his eyes had gotten darker, more greenish, and he wasn't so friendly-voiced once he'd heard Mary Anne say she was from the North.

I decided I'd better take over the talking. "We come here lookin' for a pretty black girl by the name of Delie. We don't want you to do anythin' but take us to her."

"Delie?"

His strange eyes changed again, getting wider and even deeper green. My heart sank as I saw this, and it sank even more as he said, "Delie? Our Delie? She's supposed to be *here?*"

CHAPTER FOURTEEN

The Scuppernong Cave

ELIE WASN'T HERE, AFTER ALL? I FELT SICK AT THE PIT of my stomach. In my mind I could see the rope that'd take Davey's life away.

The boy Henry asked, "Where'd you get the idea that Delie would be here? She left us with her sister and mother when the rest of the black people left. That was nearly a year ago."

I told him, "Her ma, who's livin' in a camp in Atlanta, told us she most likely would come here 'cause she's scared to stay in Atlanta."

"Scared of what?"

"Of what she saw happen there."

"What did she see?"

Mary Anne spoke up now. "We think she saw a Union Army major shot and killed in a hotel there."

"Delie saw that?"

I added now, "She was workin' at that hotel. They say my brother killed the Yankee, but I don't think he did. She left me a message that Davey didn't do it. I jest got to find her."

Henry Brackett nodded. "Get down and come inside. Talk with Papa and Mama and Boyd. Maybe they can help you. I'll get you some cold water for you and your horse if you'd like."

"Thank you. We would like that," came from Mary Anne.

Henry helped us down, Mary Anne first, then me. He was strong. He held me for a minute, looking into my face, before he let my feet touch the ground. He took Marengo to a horse trough beside the house and let him drink his fill. Then he tied the reins to a post and led us up into the house.

Where it was blazing summer outside, it was cool in there. The rooms were big and dark and almost empty of furniture. I'd always wanted to get a look into a plantation big house, but of course, as mill hands, no Reed ever got invited. Now that I was in one, I could see that there wasn't anything to it but some old, slumping-looking chairs and a little table here and there. I'd heard that there were velvet and silk draperies and rosewood and mahogany furniture in places like this before General Sherman's men came through smashing and taking whatever suited their fancy.

Three people sat together in a little room. They were playing cards. The older man and woman were gray-headed, and the young man was fair-haired with a short yellow beard. His tied-up, gray-cloth trouser leg and the crutch beside his chair told me he was one-legged. In my heart I knew the war had hurt him like it had Davey.

"Papa, Mama, Boyd, these young ladies have come from Atlanta seeking Delie," explained Henry to them. "They saw Susie, her mama, in Atlanta, and she claimed Delie must have come back here."

"Delie?" asked the older man. "She's free now. Why would she do that?"

Henry Brackett said to me, "I'm going to get you the water. You'd best tell Papa why you've come."

And so, standing beside Mary Anne, I repeated my story once again.

When I was done, Boyd Brackett said, "Delie was never a liar. Neither was her mother. I wonder where Delie did go?"

Little Mrs. Brackett, who wore a lace cap on her hair, was silent for a moment. Then, looking at me, she said, "Oh, she's here, all right. I saw her last night and gave her some food. I could see she was scared half out of her wits. Now I know why. She thanked me for the food and went away."

"Went away to where, Mother?" asked Boyd.

The woman shook her head. "You and Henry ought to know—the place where you and your brothers went when you were bad and didn't want me to find you." She turned to Henry, who had just come in with two glasses of water. "Son, you told me once that you showed your secret place to Delie, and sometimes played there with the other black children when you were small."

Henry's mouth fell open. "The cave? The old cave in the cliff under the scuppernongs?"

Mrs. Brackett sighed. "So that's where it is. After all these years I've found out."

"Yes, Mama, that's where I hid the hams and all the silver I could before the Yankees showed up. They never did get their hands on it, and I brought it all back here after they'd gone."

Mr. Brackett slapped down a card. "After they took our pigs and horses and turkeys and chickens, and burned our furniture and bedding in front of our eyes. Just before you got out of the hospital, Boyd. You came home to almost nothing."

"I came home to our land," his older son said softly. "Henry and I will make something of it again. We'll raise good cotton, and when we get ahead a bit, we'll hire workers to plant and pick it."

"Of course you and Henry will." Mrs. Brackett smiled at her sons.

I got the feeling the Bracketts had talked like this lots of times before. Henry told his ma angrily, "I could have gone to fight in Atlanta."

His father interrupted him. "You were our last boy. We lost two others and nearly lost Boyd here. I don't regret coming home from my regiment to lock you up in the smokehouse last year so you couldn't run off to defend Atlanta. We've been over this before, Henry. Now go to this secret cave of yours and see if Delie's there. If she is, fetch her back here. I want to speak with her."

"So do I," said Mrs. Brackett. "She was always a fine girl."

I couldn't help but say, "She still is. She didn't have to leave me that message."

After we'd finished our water Henry led us behind the house and over a field just full of scurrying rabbits. I couldn't see any chickens or any other live animals, so I reckoned the Bracketts lived on rabbit. Rabbit fricassee was good food the way Mama cooked it. Mr. Levy doted on it, she said.

We crossed more fields, then went up a bluff and down it over the other side. Henry shoved aside a heavy vine covered with purple scuppernong grapes at the bottom to show us the entrance to a small cave. He hollered into it, "Delie, it's Henry! Some girls have come here from Atlanta to see you. Come on out. They don't mean you any hurt. Neither does anybody here on the plantation."

We waited.

Henry sighed and went inside. He was right back, holding Delie by the wrists. She took one look at me and cried, "Hannalee."

I didn't waste any time. I told her, "Your ma told us where you would be when we went to the Decatur Road camp after you. I know what your message meant. Thank you kindly for it. You were sayin' my brother didn't kill that Yankee shoulder-straps."

Delie drew a deep breath. "Your brother didn't do that. It was the other Yankee. The soldier hit your brother so hard, he fell down and didn't know what was goin' on. The Yankee reached inside your brother's pocket and took a pistol out of it. Then the one Yankee shot the other one and set the pistol by your brother's hand. I seen it all."

My heart swelled so with joy, I couldn't say a word.

Henry asked, "How come you were there to see this, Delie?"

"I got called out of bed 'cause there was a sick-to-the-stummick lady in the hotel that needed towels and bed linens she'd messed up by throwin' up so much. They was tendin' to her, so they sent me to the linen closet at the other end of the hall from the saloon. I had a candle, but I blew it out when I heard the men fightin' and comin' my way. Nobody saw me, but I seen by the saloon light what was goin' on. I seen it, but I didn't dare tell a soul at the hotel. I don't want to be put in jail 'cause of anythin' that officer who done the killin' can say about me. I know I can't stand up in front of a judge and speak out about what my eyes saw."

"Oh, yes, you can now!" said Mary Anne.

"Who'd you be?" asked Delie. "I seen you on Peachtree Street, but I don't know your name."

"She's my friend, Mary Anne Herrick," I told her. "I work for her pa. They're Yankees, but they're good ones. Mary Anne's papa knows about the laws here. We're askin' you to come back to Atlanta with us now. Nobody'll hurt you."

Henry said, "Mama and Papa want to talk to you in the house, Delie."

Delie's eyes grew bigger, and I saw fright in them. "The menfolk at the big house is mad at me for comin' back here?"

"No, they aren't. They want to talk to you about Atlanta, that's all. Do you like it there?"

Delie's face stiffened. "The work I do is a dang sight harder, but I'm free there, where I wasn't here. I don't want to see your pa or big brother, Henry. They was soldiers for the Confederacy. I don't mind seein' your mama or you, but I don't want to see them menfolk."

I asked, "Will you please come back to Atlanta with us, Delie? Mary Anne's pa knows what he's talkin' about, and so does she. You'll be savin' my brother's life."

She told me coldly, "He was a Confederate soldier, too."

"Yes, but he's an innocent man," put in Mary Anne. "You wouldn't let an innocent person hang, would you? Your mother said you were God-fearing."

Delie frowned, thinking, then said, "No, I reckon I wouldn't. It'd be on my soul." She turned to me. "How'd you two git here?"

"On horseback," I answered.

Mary Anne said, "I suppose Marengo can carry the three of us back home."

Henry volunteered, "We haven't got a buggy anymore. Papa sold it last month for corn seed. I'd have taken you home in it if we did." He smiled. "All we've got is a mule, and he isn't carriage-broken, or saddle-broken, either."

I said, "Thank you, anyway. You been mighty good to us."

Delie went back into the cave and got her belongings. Then she and Mary Anne started out ahead of us. Although he could have walked with them up front, Henry stayed with me. He said, "Tell me about yourself, Hannalee Reed."

I took to him and his mannerliness. To my surprise I found myself telling him about my family and what we had all gone through and how we happened to be here in Atlanta.

By the time I'd finished, we were at the side of the big house. There, out of sight of Mary Anne and Delie, Henry Brackett put his hands on my shoulders and told me, "I think you have to be the bravest, as well as the prettiest, girl in all the state of Georgia. You know what? I'm going to come courting you someday, Hannalee Reed. You remember that. I'll come looking for you in Atlanta, and I'll find you."

Then he touched my hair. "You've got the shiniest, blackest hair I've ever seen."

The honest words leapt out of my mouth. "It ain't all mine. Part of it's my mama's. Remember, I told you I cut off my braids to save my little brother?"

"It doesn't matter. By the time I come for you, it'll be grown long enough for you to sit on the way a lady's hair ought to be."

Now he bent his head and kissed me—not on the cheek but softly on the lips.

There wasn't one word for me to say. I'd never had such a thing happen to me. I'd never met such an exciting boy. Mill-hand boys I'd known didn't talk or act one bit like he did.

"You'd all best get back to Atlanta before it gets dark," he said now.

Mary Anne and Delie were already mounted. Henry lifted me up behind Delie, and I put my arms around her waist, holding on tight. She was thin and so was I. There was still a little empty place on the horse's rump.

"Thank you," Mary Anne told Henry.

He said to Delie, "Don't worry. You'll be all right." To me he said, "Bear in mind what I told you, Hannalee."

Bear it in mind? I'd remember all my life what he said, even if I never set eyes on him again. He thought I was brave, and pretty, too. Maybe he would come hunting me someday. Stranger things had happened in my life.

Henry stood for a long time watching us leave. I kept my head turned until I couldn't see the white blur that was his shirt anymore. My neck ached when I brought my head back to stare at the nape of Delie's neck.

The cloth bag she carried her belongings in swung back and forth from her wrist all the way to Atlanta, banging me on the right knee. I didn't care, though. There was a singing in my soul. Davey'd be all right now. What Delie could say would save him. Mary Anne and Delie and I saved him, and Henry Brackett, too, by taking us to the scuppernong cave. I'd never look at another scuppernong without remembering him and his kiss. I reckoned a girl's first kiss from a boy would be one thing she'd never forget in her whole life. Did boys remember their first kiss, too?

When we were on Decatur Road again, Mary Anne called back over her shoulder, "We have to take Delie to her mother's house first to let her know Delie's safe. Then we'll take her to Papa where it'll be better for her."

Delie jerked, then said, "No, I want to be with Ma and Lucy."

"I been thinkin' on that along the way," I told her. "Mebbe that Yankee you saw shoot the major might get an idea somebody saw him do that. He could be lookin' for you, Delie, knowin' you ran off that very night and askin' questions from hotel folks."

I felt Delie shiver. "All right, I'll only let Ma see me,

and then I'll come back with you." She asked Mary Anne, "Will I be all right where you live?"

"You'll be fine. Papa will be happy to have you. He'll figure out how to handle things for you."

I added now, "My mama will talk to the man she works for, too. He knows plenty about the law."

Delie said, "But the man who shot that officer is a Yankee, too!"

Mary Anne told her, "No matter. When they have to, Yankees hang other Yankees. They do it to criminals up where I come from. Nobody decent takes pleasure from it, but grown-ups sometimes say it has to be done to protect everybody from truly dangerous people."

I asked out loud, "Why would a Yankee shoulder-straps shoot another one?"

Delie answered me, "I dunno, but I heard 'em usin' a girl's name."

I asked, "Was the name Amalie?"

"That's it—or mebbe Emily."

I said, "It was Amalie, and that most likely was the reason for the shootin'. Jealousy!"

It did my heart good to see how glad Delie's ma and sister were to see her again. They hugged and kissed, and then they listened to what Mary Anne had to say about taking Delie to Atlanta. They agreed that she should go and helped her back onto Marengo, this time behind us.

The sun was just setting when we got to the Herricks' store. The minute we rode up on Marengo, Mr. Herrick came boiling out the back door the way I figured he might.

He shouted at Mary Anne, "If you were a boy, I'd whip the daylights out of you! Where have you been all this time? What have you been up to? What are you doing with this black girl? I've been worried out of my wits."

After saying all that he calmed down a bit the way mamas and papas generally did once they'd let the steam out of their engines.

Mary Anne told him, "Papa, please help us down. We're just fine. We've been doing a good deed, but now we're tired and hungry. This is Delie. She'll be staying with us for a little while. She saw who truly shot the major at the hotel. I said you'd look after her. I promised her."

"What? *Who* shot him?" demanded Mr. Herrick.

"That other Yankee officer, Papa."

I saw Mary Anne's father swallow hard. He nodded just once, held up his arms, and lifted first Delie, then me, then Mary Anne down. After that he told us, "Mary Anne, you and Delie get inside right now and stay there while I tend to the horse. You, Hannalee, go home at once."

I told him, "All us Reeds is sorry to cause you so much trouble. If you don't want me to, I won't come back to work tomorrow. I'll understand."

"I'll expect you at the same time as usual. Now get

home as fast as you can. Run! The city's disturbed because of the murder. Other things have happened since you and Mary Anne left at noon."

"What? They didn't hang my brother?" I cried.

"No, it isn't that. Get along with you, Hannalee. Ask your family to tell you any news they might have. Doesn't your little brother work for the newspaper? He ought to be able to tell you."

I didn't wait any longer. Though I was sore in my behind from all that horseback riding, I lit out for home and Mama at the best run I could manage. One glance over my shoulder showed me Mr. Herrick taking Marengo's saddle off and the back door closing behind Mary Anne and Delie.

Oh, but I had a mouthful of news to tell Mama, Jem, and Aunt Marilly. Their eyes would bug out of their faces and they'd weep for joy!

CHAPTER FIFTEEN

We Do Things!

THEY WERE ALL THERE TOGETHER IN OUR SHACK LIKE they were waiting for me to come home.

Before I could get out a word about my afternoon's work, Jem jumped up from his stool. "Hannalee, did you hear the news? The bluebelly soldiers caught Mr. Redmond thirty miles north of here this mornin'. They put him in jail sayin' he's one of the Regulators. Folks he's robbed and beaten up recognized his face."

I asked, "What about Davey? How's he?"

Mama answered, "He's still where he was."

Mama was on a mattress, with Paulina kicking up her heels beside her like she didn't have a care in the world. Aunt Marilly was sitting in the chair Davey had made out of some sticks and rope. That left me the other stool.

I was weary and sat down on it. But before I could get my brains in order to start my tale, Jem went on yelling, "Gar says he dropped the pistol he'd been carryin' into Davey's pocket so he wouldn't shoot the bluebelly shoulder-straps Major Fenton, hisself. Redmond had jest found out that the Yankee was married to a wife up north

and was courtin' Miz Amalie all the same. He was even
talkin' to her about marryin' him. Gar run out of the hotel
before he lost hold of hisself and shot that Yankee." Jem's
mouth twisted. "He says he told Davey the bluebelly was
already wed, and he thinks mebbe Davey shot him."

Now it was my turn to talk. "It don't matter one bit
what Mr. Gar Redmond thinks or has to say. Davey
didn't shoot nobody. I know it and I can prove it!"

"*You*, Hannalee? You can?" Mama picked Paulina up
and held her tight.

"You bet. I wasn't measurin' and cuttin' yard goods at
Mr. Herrick's most of today at all. I had myself a journey
with his daughter, Mary Anne." Sitting back in content-
ment with my hands on my knees, I told my family how
the two of us had found Delie, and what she had to say
about the shooting.

Mama's eyes appeared to be on fire, she was so full of
joy. Her and Marilly's and Jem's faces were streaked with
tears—and mine, too.

When I finished, Mama shook her head. "You could
have had terrible things happen to you girls. Well, I will
say you hung the moon in the sky agin, Hannalee. The
black girl left you words marked down in your book, and
you understood 'em, and you and this Yankee girl were
off like a shot."

Aunt Marilly, who'd wiped her eyes with the hem of
her dress, suddenly looked straight at me and cried out,

"Wait a minute! A black can't stand up in court and speak out aginst a white man."

Folding my arms the way grown-ups do when they're sure of themselves, I said, "Oh, yes, they can! Mary Anne's pa said under Yankee law, which is the kind we got here right now, they can."

Mama leaned back against the wall and gave out a sort of weak laugh. "I never thought I'd ever say any Yankee doin's would please me, but that day has come and I bless it." She handed Paulina to Marilly with the words, "I'm puttin' on my hat and shawl and goin' back to Mr. Levy right this minute. Hannalee, you come with me to tell him what you jest told us."

Suddenly I felt a hole in my innards big enough to pitch a dog through, I was so hungry from all my riding and running. I asked, "Will he feed me? I feel sort of feeble."

"I fried him a rabbit today. There ought to be some left over from his supper for the two of us. I talked to him about Davey today, and he said for my sake he'd try to be helpful however he could."

As we left, I told Mama, "If it's true that a angel foots up a person's account on Judgment Day, Mary Anne Herrick ought to have lots of stars in her crown—she was so helpful to me today."

Later, while I ate cold fried rabbit, I told my story to Mr. Levy. He listened without saying one single word, only now and then writing something I said down on the paper he had beside him.

When I'd ended, he said, "That's a most commendable enterprise for you and this Herrick child to have accomplished."

"What does all them big words mean, sir?"

"That you two did a very good thing, but you should have taken a responsible adult with you."

I told him, "Mary Anne says they can fiddle-faddle around too long some of the time. We got done what had to be done fast."

I saw him hide a smile with his hand.

Mama asked him, "What should we do now, Mr. Levy?"

"Wait till morning. Then we'll all go to see Mr. Herrick and this Delie and talk. Then I suspect we'll all go together to the provost marshal's office."

I cried out, "Delie won't like that! After what she saw, she's scared of that Yankee officer."

He nodded his silvery head. "She has cause to be, but no one will harm her."

Our talk with Mr. Levy wasn't the only one that took place that night. On the way back home, Mama and I ran smack-dab into Miz Amalie sitting in a canvas-top wagon driven by a Yankee sergeant. At first we didn't know her. Her head was covered by the hood of her cloak, but she let it fall back when she spotted us abreast of her on the street.

She spoke to the soldier, who halted the horses, then she got down over the wheel to come up to us.

She told us, "I'm saying good-bye to you folks now. I hoped I'd get to see you before I went away, but I couldn't come to your camp. I'm leaving, going to Macon or maybe Savannah later on." I saw by the torchlight of somebody passing by that her face was pulled tight by strain and that her eyes were a-glitter. She went on, "You know Gar's in jail and that he's a Regulator. God knows, I didn't want him to be one, but he never once listened to me. He'll say I ran away when he needed me most, but when I had need of him, he'd be gone most of the time. This time I'm the one to go! The war will never be over in Gar's mind. I know that. I'm sorry he got your Davey mixed up in all this. He'd mix up anybody Southern he could. I thought I could have come to love your son, Miz Reed, but after a time I could see his heart had been bestowed elsewhere."

Mama told her softly, "I'm sorry for you, Miz Amalie."

Miz Redmond got out a hard laugh. "I wasn't ever cut out to be a fine lady who married and settled down and had a family and never said or did anything that would upset her family. All I ever learned was petit point and to play the spinet and write a little poetry. I was never allowed to drive my own buggy or cook anything but candy. I could only dance in ballrooms in white lace wrist-let gloves, flirt and smile, smile, smile, until my face ached. I thought sometimes I was strangling in an old closet. The only man I ever thought I might marry was killed at Chancellorsville. My business and the Yankees were the fresh air I needed. I worked hard. I made money. Atlanta women hate me because I was a friend to some Yankees, but I had to be to keep my store going."

Mama asked, "What'll you do now?"

"Soon as I can, I'll start up another candy store even if I'm a woman alone. I've got some money to do that. It's all I know. I won't ever come back here. I have to leave now. The sergeant's waiting. My Yankee friends say I'd best leave before somebody attacks me or my store. They sent soldiers to help me pack and left more to guard my store, and later on they'll see to it that I get a fair price for it from a new owner. Good-bye to you now. Good luck to all of you."

And she left us. We saw her helped up onto the seat by the hand of the sergeant, who now drove off.

Mama and I stood staring after her as the wagon went on its way south. Finally Mama shook her head and told us, "It can't ever be easy bein' a woman alone tryin' to swim upstream aginst the current. Women have a mighty task in this world that men set up and rule over. I do believe I understand Miz Amalie now, and I bear her no malice in my heart over Davey's sore troubles."

I said, "I don't, either, Mama."

★   ★   ★

Though Mr. Levy had a carriage house out behind his big house, he didn't keep a horse or buggy. He walked over the next day, the way we did, to meet with us, the Herricks, and Delie in back of the cloth-goods store.

Delie seemed to be easier in her mind than yesterday. She told everybody what she'd seen, smooth as silk. Then Mr. Levy said, "My child, we're going to be taking you to the provost marshal here in Atlanta. Will you tell him what you just told us?"

"Yes, sir, I will. Can my mama be there when I do?"

"Not today, I'm afraid. Don't be frightened."

"All right, I won't. I ain't scared no more now that there's two of you men Yankees to go with me." She asked, "Will I get my job back at the hotel later on?"

Mr. Levy nodded and said, "I do believe Mr. Herrick and I can arrange that for you."

So Delie and the two men left, one on each side of her, for the provost marshal's office. That left Mama and me and Mary Anne alone. Mama went back to our camp to wait with Marilly and Paulina for news from Mr. Levy. Mary Anne went out to currycomb Marengo. I closed up the store. I had something to do that I'd been thinking on since meeting up with Miz Amalie yesterday evening.

Trying to look braver than I felt, I walked to the court-house lawn where the bluebellies had put up all their tents and huts. It sure wasn't any place for a Rebel to walk into, but I had to do it. I just had to!

When the first guard stopped me, I told him, "I'm lookin' for Lieutenant Marcus Burton of the Indiana cavalry. Do you know him or where his unit might be livin' here?"

The soldier laughed and gave me directions to go down a long, long line of tents. Men in blue were everywhere, lolling about smoking pipes, playing cards, reading, and darning socks. All of them stared hard at me as I passed.

I heard one say, "What's that little goober grabber doing here?"

I stopped and said, "This goober eater's lookin' for a Lieutenant Marcus Burton in the Indiana cavalry."

"Won't the infantry do, little girl?" asked another man, blowing me a kiss.

"No, I need the cavalry."

How they laughed at that, and my face flamed with embarrassment.

Finally a tall red-headed Yankee sergeant offered to be my guide. He led me to some tents, called out Lieutenant Burton's name, and out came my soldier. Somebody from inside yelled, "Marcus, she's too young for you. Throw her back in the pond for a couple of years."

He looked amazed to see me and said, "Hannalee, what are you doing here? If it's about your soldier brother, I can't help him."

Well, I'd reckoned he'd know about that soon. Everybody in Atlanta who read the *Intelligencer* would.

I said, "I didn't come about that. It's about somethin' else. Have you had any letters from your mama lately?"

"Yes, as a matter of fact, I got one yesterday. My letter to her about finding you crossed hers in the mail. She'll be glad to hear you made it home all right."

I said, "Please, did she say anythin' in her letter about a girl up there by the name of Rosellen?"

"Why, yes, she did. Here, I've got the letter in my pocket. Do you want me to read to you what she wrote?"

"I'd be mighty obliged."

He took out the sheets of paper, looked them over, and read, " 'Rosellen, who lives here with me, hopes you can find the child you are seeking and that all is well. This girl herself, Marcus, is the source of some worry to me. She's not as well as she once was. She's put away her pretty shawl and hair combs and gowns. All she'll wear now is black. I have reason to believe she's in mourning. She received a letter last winter, the contents of which she never shared with me. She keeps it folded in a silver locket on a black ribbon. She constantly wears this locket. My other mill-hand boarders have all gone home to the South now. Only Rosellen remains, and I'm glad of her company, but I worry over her as I would over a daughter. To change the subject, I have a cat and some kittens now, pretty little soft gray ones, to keep me company while I wait for you and your brother to get out of the Army.' That's all there is about the girl called Rosellen."

That was enough. It was just what I needed. I told him, "Thank you kindly. You read me what I wanted to hear."

He said, "Did I? Do you know who Rosellen's grieving for?"

"Uh-huh, for my big brother. She thinks he's dead, but he isn't. That's my letter she has in the locket she wears."

"Maybe I'd better write Mother that he's still alive?"

I touched his hand. "Please don't do that. My brother wants her to think he got killed in a battle 'cause he's one-armed now. Don't mention us Reeds no more."

"All right, I won't. That's a pity. I'm sorry to hear about his arm, Hannalee, and I'm sorry about the trouble he's in right now."

I felt I'd done my errand now, so I held out my hand and shook his big, hard brown one. Then I turned on my heel and walked back through the Yankee camp, not caring how often I heard the name "goober grabber" called after me. I had plenty to think on now.

We never found out what went on in the provost marshal's office, because none of us Reeds were invited to hear the goings-on that continued for the next few days.

Mama went to visit Davey and told him what Delie had seen and Mary Anne and I had done, and what Mr. Levy and Mr. Herrick were up to now. She said he was greatly bucked up by it and proud as could be of me.

As for us Reeds and Aunt Marilly, we went on working

and praying and hoping that the Yankees would believe Delie over their own captain. We didn't see Delie once. She'd been sent to live in a Yankee officer's house for extra protection.

A week went by, a long, hard one with all of us waiting and waiting.

And then one evening—Monday night, it was—Davey came walking into our shack. We jumped all over him, crying and laughing and hugging him.

He told us, "The word ain't gotten around yet in town, but the bluebelly captain shot hisself in the chest two days back. He's real bad off in a hospital. Nobody knowed why he did such a thing till that brave little gal was brought in to see him face-to-face in his hospital room. In front of him and everybody else she told him what she'd seen him do. The captain come out with the truth then, sayin' he was drunk enuf and crazy enuf with jealousy to shoot Major Fenton over Amalie Redmond. He was jealous of me, too, 'cause I squired her some. The captain saw Gar Redmond put his pistol in my pocket but didn't do anythin' about it then. He was waitin' for his chance. He got it later on when he hit me, took out Gar's pistol, shot the major with it, and set it down beside me. That's what the black girl said she saw, too. If Hartford lives, they'll hang him."

Mama asked, "What about Mr. Redmond?"

"They're goin' to bring him to trial as a Regulator. He

should have run off to Mexico or Brazil like he said he might. They planned to try me as a Regulator, too, but I said that I never was one. Gar backed me up. He told 'em I was asked to join but that I'd said no. And nobody ever said they saw a one-armed man with any night riders." Davey laughed. "So somethin' good's come out of bein' one-armed, after all. Folks notice you. Now I'm free as a bird and can go back to telegraph work." He grinned at me. "I sure owe you plenty, Hannalee, for all you done for me."

I said, "You don't owe nothin'. I did it out of fam'ly affection."

Mama told him with a sigh, "Davey, I'm glad you never rode with Redmond. We sort of suspicioned you did some nights."

"No, I only went to one meetin', and that night I come back here in a buggy. Most nights they went ridin', I stayed by myself drinkin'. I'm weary of trouble. That's why I'll be glad to git back to the telegraph key."

All at once Mama said something that made us all suck in our breath. "Mr. Levy wants to know if you'd like to carpenter some and fix up his carriage house for us to live in this winter. He said he don't want me to have to walk so far to get to his place in bad weather."

"I reckon I could do that in my time off from telegraph work. It'd be a lot more useful to all us Reeds than feelin' sorry for myself so much."

Well, Mama had surely kept this fine secret to herself till Davey came back home, hadn't she?

And I was just busting to tell mine. I said fast, "Davey, I got somethin' to tell you—somethin' you're gonna have to make up your mind about. You'd best sit down first. Jem, give him the stool you're on now. Davey, I have good cause to think your true love's still true to you. No, don't you look mad at me like that! Set still and lemme tell you what I got to say."

Walking on my way to work the next morning, I thought I must have glowed rosy-red with pure happiness. I was pretty sure Rosellen'd come back home with Davey— after some argument with him about this and that once they'd had their first hello-again hugs and kisses over with.

Thinking of them two so loving made me think of somebody else, and I felt my cheeks getting hot. Henry Brackett's kissing me on the lips hadn't been no chicken peck of a kiss. It'd been the kind a prince gives the fairy-tale princess to wake her up from a wicked spell she was under. Yep, I reckoned Henry would climb through brambles up a tower to give me a kiss if I was in an enchanted slumber.

Maybe there was something to fairy tales and the old, sad ballads about true lovers, after all. Look at Davey's and Rosellen's love. That could be a ballad. He was her prince, and she was his lady fair.

Was I, Hannalee Reed, black-haired Hannalee, Henry Brackett's lady fair? He seemed to think I was, even if all fairy-tale ladies had golden heads like Rosellen.

I spent all the rest of that day deep in comforting dreams of his kiss. I could feel him near me while I was measuring and cutting cloth, thinking on me, too. I knew I'd see him again! Maybe my Indian blood was coming out, telling me what was to come, like it did for Mama. If that was so, I told it "Welcome."

Two days after Davey took the train north to claim Rosellen in Indiana, I went over to the Beaufort Hotel to visit Delie. She did get her old job back, just like Mr. Herrick and Mr. Levy promised. I reckoned she'd stay there till she got something that would suit her better.

I found her out behind the hotel pegging towels on the clothesline. "Hello, Delie," I called to her.

"Hello, Hannalee," she said with a wooden clothes peg between her teeth.

I took my fairy-tale book from under my arm and held it out to her. "You never did get to finish this."

"I reckon you're right. I never did."

"Would you like a loan of it agin?"

"I reckon so."

"I'll go put it on the back steps for you where it won't get wet from all them damp towels."

"Thank you, Hannalee."

"Thank you, Delie, for what you did for our Davey."

"I done my duty. That's all."

"Mary Anne wants you to come over noontime sometimes so she can help you with your readin' when she helps me. She's real good at that. Will you come?"

Delie gave me a tiny little smile. "Mebbe so. Tell her thank you, too."

"I'll be sure to do that." And I turned around and headed for the Herricks's and my work again. Oh, what would the good Lord send us next year? I asked myself as I walked along.

Author's Note

TO MY KNOWLEDGE THERE HAS NEVER BEEN A BOOK FOR young readers dealing with the poor whites and blacks in the rebuilding of Atlanta. I hope in this to pay homage to all the Hannalees, Jems, Daveys, and Delies.

It is fact that only four hundred or so houses out of some four thousand were left standing in Atlanta after the Yankee general William T. Sherman set fire to the city. The city actually burned three times—first as a result of Yankee incendiary bombs, then by the Confederates destroying ammunition cars, and finally as a result of Sherman's orders. After he left Atlanta he sent his huge army on a fifty-mile-wide swath through Georgia, burning and taking the possessions of rural residents and townspeople. To this day he is detested by some Georgians for his ruthless cruelty. However, to give him some credit, he proclaimed that his treatment of Georgia was to hasten the end of the Civil War.

What I have written here of the refugee camps for the white people and the blacks is true. The camps were separate and miles apart. Though both camps had unhealthy locales, smallpox raged among the blacks so recently delivered from slavery but was not found in the white camp.

Martial law ruled in Atlanta in 1865. Passes were required. Strict military order was kept, though surely it had some real failures. At the end of 1865, Atlanta's population was estimated at ten thousand. To demonstrate the violence of the town in this one year, there were thirty-one killings, forty-three shootings, and fifty-five beatings. In 1865, Atlanta was like Western gold camps, a boomtown. Prices were shockingly high for the bare necessities of life. The Neal House, Sherman's headquarters, was a real place. My Beaufort Hotel is based on the old Planters' Hotel.

The secret Southern organization called the Ku Klux Klan supposedly began in 1867. Prior to that, Georgians in Atlanta who resented Yankee rule and black freedom banded together as "Regulators," riding by night to beat blacks they met on the road. Other riders were simple bandits and gangs of army deserters—North and South— who specialized in highway robbery and horse theft, and owed loyalty to no one but themselves.

It may seem odd that my formerly wealthy Atlantans, the Redmonds, operate a candy store. The candy business was actually one of the most important ones in 1865 by record. Men who had never before worked with their hands now did so. Women who had never worked at all were forced to in order to support their families. They did what they could, selling homemade cakes and candy. Besides, with the Yankee sea blockade lifted, sugar could come in from the Caribbean again, and the Southerners were starved for something sweet other than honey or molasses.

Georgia's plantation owners found difficulty in commencing to grow cotton after the Civil War. Slavery had been abolished, and the blacks had scattered, so they needed to find workers who would be paid wages. Having backed the war effort financially, many landowners had little money to pay them with. Plantations in the swath General Sherman cut across the state suffered most of all because Union soldiers burned the houses, barns, stables, and cotton processing machinery. Some landowners in parts of Georgia sold off property to keep going. Some were forced to sell to Yankees. Others managed with free slave workers, often elderly, who had never left the plantations or, disliking town life, had drifted back to them because this was a place they knew.

Most Atlanta girls steered clear of flirtations with Union Army soldiers out of patriotism and respect for Southern men. However, flirtation was a natural thing between young and lonely Union soldiers and Atlanta's girls, and it went on, though greatly disapproved of by older people. Some marriages took place, which left the Southern wife open to snubs from her former friends, who never would forgive her.

Among Southern cities, Atlanta has always held an unusual place. It seems to have been considered the New York City of the prewar era because of its feverish activity. Unlike Savannah, New Orleans, Charleston, and other Southern cities, it was still a new town in 1865. When General Sherman burned it, it was only some thirty years old. Even today Atlanta is known for its progressiveness and is a hub of business enterprise. Very little remains of the city from pre–Civil War days.

THE BLACKS

Only two years away from slavery, the black citizens of Atlanta would not have found living easy. Many had come off the plantations to live in the Decatur Road refugee camp. Though they would have been able to get food supplies through the Yankee-operated Freedman's Bureau, they would have had to compete with whites for jobs.

It is true that by prewar Georgia law, no black could testify in court against a white person, though he or she could testify against another black. Former slaves had a natural fear of white men's law processes, so Delie's fleeing would not have been an odd thing for her to do. Nor would her strong religious bent be strange. Many Southern blacks, though they were not taught to read and write, were taught religion. It is a fact that ex-slaves hungered for education. When schools for blacks were started in Georgia, four generations of the same family might be in the same classroom. Laundresses and other workers propped the ABCs up before them at their work. Black schools began in the 1860s in Atlanta, before schools for white children started again in the early 1870s. Schools for white children prior to the Civil War had been private ones requiring tuition. It is also a fact that many freed slaves took the names of their former owners as their own surnames.

Two rumors were current in the black society in late 1865. One was that the federal government would divide all the land in the Southern states by the end of the year and give it to them along with the means to farm it. This, of course, was wishful thinking. The other was that the blacks were being lured by offers of work by white Southerners to seaports, forced onto ships, and sold as slaves in Cuba. I cannot verify this. However, it is true that Cuba, then under the rule of Spain, did not abolish slavery by royal decree until 1887. Isolated cases of the sale of American blacks could have taken place, though the histories of Cuba I looked into make no mention of this.

There is a shyness in my book between Hannalee and the black girl, Delie, and a great dislike on Delie's part of Confederate soldiers. Had the South won the war, she would have stayed a slave. As a former slave, I believe she would have been on guard as to Hannalee's intentions toward her. There must have been a great deal of suspicion, if not downright hostility, between some ex-slaves and their former owners. Though my Reed family, like many other Southerners, were not and had never been slaveholders, they would have felt this wariness, too. It would have been quite normal. Freedom was very new to the blacks. The memory of their bondage and mistreatment was very fresh in their minds. The wisest of them may have known that their road ahead would be long and difficult— as it was. They had a hundred-year wait until the 1960s Civil Rights Movement began to focus on blacks moving forward with pride into the American mainstream.

MARTIAL LAW

Martial law is called for in special and difficult situations where ordinary policing is not thought adequate to control trouble. It can be imposed by states' governors in the case of rioting, revolt, earthquakes, flooding, etc., or by presidents in national emergencies. Soldiers keep the order. Living under martial law is unpleasant. Citizens often require passes or papers to prove their identity and must report where their business is taking them. Curfews are generally set up for night hours. In normal times police need a warrant to search a house or must have legal papers for some cause to arrest a person. Under martial law no warrants or papers are needed. Soldiers can arrest simply on suspicion. Most trials held under martial law—even of civilians—are military trials. (Davey Reed, if his case came to court, would have been tried by soldiers, though civilians could be called to speak as witnesses. There were a number of such trials of civilians under martial law after the Civil War.)

GEORGIA

Georgia, which had become a state in 1788, seceded from the Union in January 1861, to join the Confederacy. The battles of Chickamauga, Resaca, Pine Mountain, Kennesaw Mountain, Peachtree Creek, Atlanta, and Jonesboro were fought inside its boundaries.

Its post–Civil War history was stormy, to say the least. In 1865, a state convention repealed the Secession Ordinance, and in December of that year the legislature ratified the Thirteenth Amendment to the U.S. Constitution, the one abolishing slavery.

The state now had to have a new constitution of its own. While still under Yankee martial law, its convention met in Atlanta late in 1867. This was the time, too, that the infamous Ku Klux Klan, a racist and violence-prone organization that insisted on secrecy, made its first appearance. It continues its activities into the present day.

In early 1868, the constitutional convention adopted a new state constitution. At this time, too, the capital was moved from Milledgeville to Atlanta. In July, the state legislature ratified the Fourteenth Amendment, which gave equal protection of U.S. law to all persons regardless of race. Now civil government was restored.

The year 1869 witnessed the Georgia legislature rejecting the Fifteenth Amendment, the one that would give the vote to black men. Martial law was once more imposed. (Before this rejection, white men elected to the legislature had refused to let elected black men take their seats.)

In 1870, the legislature ratified the Fifteenth Amendment to the U.S. Constitution and reratified the Fourteenth. Now Georgia was admitted to the Union.

Economic conditions were very hard in the state after the Civil War. The huge cotton plantations were broken up into smaller sections of land. Because the planters had no money to pay workers, they began to use sharecropping and tenant farming, which many people disliked for these systems' inefficiency and exploitation.

When 1900 rolled around, Georgia was still chiefly agricultural, with a heavy emphasis on cotton farming, which exhausts the land, but also grew peanuts and fruits and vegetables, and raised cattle.

Today's Georgia is quite different from Hannalee Reed's state—or even the state as it was in 1900. An infestation of insects hit cotton farming hard in the 1920s. Land once given over to cotton is now grazing land and forest.

Twentieth-century Georgia is more industrial than agricultural. It manufactures textiles and paper products. Atlanta is a very important commercial city and national center for conventions.

In the 1960s, the Reverend Martin Luther King, Jr., and the Civil Rights Movement were active in the state. In

1970, Georgia gave the Union a native son and civil rights backer, Jimmy Carter, as our United States president. Three years later Atlanta elected a black mayor, something undreamed of in Civil War times.

In writing this novel I have dealt with much background material that has come to me from a number of universities. The Atlanta Historical Society was most helpful in sending me books and pamphlets and suggesting special works such as Franklin M. Garrett's detailed history of Atlanta. My Carolinas-born friend, Faye Dunkle, read my manuscript for old-time Southern speech.

As always, people on the faculty and staff of the University of California, Riverside, are to be thanked for aid given me. I owe gratitude to Dr. Milton Miller and Dr. H. Frank Way for the help they gave me on the subject of martial law, and on this topic I must also thank Colonel Phillip W. Robbins, U.S. Army (retired). When it comes to the University of California, Riverside, library staff, I wish to thank Marie Genung, Ruth Holman, Peter Bliss, and Nancy Huling, who aided me when specific problems arose by telling me where to look for possible answers. I also wish to thank Billie E. Dancy of the Riverside Public Library for reading the manuscript.

—Patricia Beatty
July 1987